Prickly-Pong Island

&

The Revenge of Captain Red

Christopher

Davies

FOR

Mark and Izzy

Author's Note

This is the second title in the Prickly-Pong Island Series, but it can be read as a standalone book. The first title in the series is called, 'Prickly-Pong Island & the Emerald Treasure' and it is available from Kenilworth Books and Amazon.

Some of the names and locations in this book are factual, but all of the characters and events are fictitious.

Thank you

I would like to thank a few special people who have helped me in the publication of this book.

Firstly I would to say thank you to Merryn for all her help with editing and feedback. I would also like to say a big thank you to Megan (graphic designer) for all her help with the cover design.

I would also like to say a special thank you to Judy at Kenilworth Books for all her help and marketing advice.

Finally, I would like to reserve a massive thank you to you, the reader, for choosing this book. I hope you enjoy it.

Chapter 1

Missing Minoo

"Scurvy dogs!" bellowed Captain Red furiously, as he swished his long silver cutlass through the fresh morning air. "Hand me that treasure map NOW, or you and your monkey friend will be joining the sharks for breakfast!"

"Never!" I replied, defiantly. "It's Takootu's treasure – not yours."

The Captain let out a sinister laugh and chased us terrifyingly close to the edge of the cliff, where a wooden plank was sticking out over the precipice...

Minoo gripped on to me tightly.

We could see ravenous sharks circling in the ocean below.

"PLANK! PLANK! PLANK!" shouted the mob of despicable pirates.

"Start walking…" snarled the Captain, menacingly.

I hugged Minoo close to me. His heart was racing even faster than mine.

There was no way out for us this time…

"Try to concentrate please, Jay" sighed Mrs Mason my class teacher. "You've been staring at the white board for a whole minute."

"Sorry Miss," I replied, suddenly feeling VERY relieved that I was in the middle of a maths lesson and not about to be forced off a cliff into the ocean.

"You will be sorry, if you have to stay in at break time again to finish." replied Mrs Mason, dryly.

I had lost LOADS of my break times recently to catch up with my work. I just couldn't help it. After last year's amazing adventure on a desert island, I found it almost impossible to concentrate – ALL of my school work seemed so dreary and DULL!

"Remember to multiply the numerators of both fractions – then multiply the denominators…" continued Mrs Mason, pointing to an example on the board.

I just day-dreamed through ALL of my lessons wondering about Minoo, my magical monkey friend. I really missed him. I kept imagining I was back there on our island, climbing giant palm trees together, playing tig on the beach and escaping with Zeo's Treasure from Captain Red and his blood-thirsty pirates...

"Anyone who hasn't finished by the end of the lesson WILL be joining me at break time." glared Mrs Mason, noticing my blank page as she passed by.

There were twenty problems on the white board and I was still stuck on number one. It looked like I definitely WOULD be keeping Miss company at break time... AGAIN!

I couldn't wait to get back out to Zeo, our beautiful island in the South Pacific. To see Minoo and Takootu and have more wonderful adventures...

Chapter 2

Jedi-Masters

The school year went by SO slowly. The one day I really enjoyed was when it was time for Sanjana and me to do our 'Show and Tell'. Smith, our surname, was almost last on the register so we had to wait ages for our turn.

Sanjana, for those of you who don't know, is my older twin sister who absolutely loves school (unlike me). Sanjana knows everything about everything, which can get really annoying at times, especially as we are in the same class and she is actually ONLY 11 minutes older than me!

But having a super-smart sister can also come in very handy, as I found out last year on our desert island adventure.

Sanjana, who now likes to be called Jana for some reason, was first to show. She took in her sketch book which was full of her beautiful butterfly drawings from our desert island. Mrs Mason and the class were really impressed. I was too. She really is a fantastic artist, almost as good as Mum, but don't tell Jana I said that!

Next, we showed them the Rodu that Takootu, the Chief of the Radi, had presented us with as a gift for finding Zeo's Treasure.

"Wow! What are those?" demanded Jake, excitedly.

We explained that Takootu's people (who were called Radi) used them as weapons to protect themselves, and that they were carved from the trunks of palm trees from the sacred island of Radimatu.

"They look really cool!" yelled Mo, from the back of the room.

We gave the class a quick demonstration of how to use the Rodu in a mock fight. We had kept up our training like Takootu had asked us to do, and were both quite confident now at attacking and defending. I pretended to be Takootu and Jana reluctantly agreed to be Captain Red. The class loved it.

"They're battling like Jedi-masters!" shouted Max.

"Can I have a go?" asked Millie, excitedly.

We let all the class come up in turn and try them out. They didn't want to stop, but Miss was looking worried that someone might get bashed on the head so we had to finish. There was a big sigh of disappointment from the class, but I had one more thing left to show. I took out Grandad's battered telescope.

"What's that old thing?" asked one of my best friends, Fin.

We went on to tell them all about our adventure and how the telescope had really helped us. First, to spot the pirates out at sea, so we had time to hide up the giant palms. Then, how Takootu had used it as a weapon to battle off Captain Red and save us all from walking the plank and being eaten by the sharks! The class listened on, almost spellbound.

"You could have been KILLED!" cried Neela, looking very concerned.

"Yes," agreed Jana, solemnly. "It was extremely scary – even worse than the night my annoying brother hid a big black spider in my bed cabin!"

The class started to laugh, but Jana wasn't amused. She turned around and looked daggers at me – she STILL hadn't forgotten about it.

"But there were fun parts too…" I smirked, cheerfully.

"Oh yes," replied Jana, excitedly, as though she had just remembered some really embarrassing story about me. "The day JAY fell out of the tree!"

The class roared with laughter.

She then went on to tell them about the day I was pretending to be a monkey with Minoo and I fell right out of the palm trees into a huge patch of Prickly-Pong!

"What's Prickly-Pong?" laughed Max.

Jana explained that Prickly-Pong was the name we had given to a peculiar little plant that was growing all over our island. It had masses of extremely sharp thorns on its stem and the scent coming from the flowers was repulsive.

"OUCH!" shouted Fin.

"POOH!" chuckled Max, pulling a horrible face.

"That's why you named it Prickly-Pong," beamed Millie.

"Exactly," replied Jana, with a big smile. "Jay had nasty cuts all over him and he smelt like a stink bomb for more than a week!"

The class sniggered again.

It was great fun telling them all about our wonderful Gigantuki Island. They were such happy memories - even the painful ones. But then we went on to tell them the really sad part of our adventure. About how our beautiful island had been taken over by the giant Prickly-Pong and how Minoo had almost died from his wounds.

"But I don't understand. Why did the Prickly-Pong grow so big?" asked Isabel, inquisitively.

We explained to them about Dad cutting down all the trees to build a raft and how the extra light made the tiny thistle-like Prickly-Pong grow out of control.

"It was a nightmare," cried Jana, emotionally. "Our pretty little Prickly-Pong transformed into giant monstrous plants with thorns like razor blades! Our beautiful desert island was completely destroyed."

"Your parents should have listened to your concerns." said Max, seriously. "Adults always think they know best."

I thought Miss was going to say something after this

last remark, but she didn't. She seemed totally engrossed, just like the others.

The class listened on and asked us loads more questions about it. I'm not sure if they believed everything we had told them, but we knew it was all true, even though it sounded almost unbelievable when we were telling them.

What's more, we knew that in a matter of weeks we would be back out there with Takootu and Minoo, having more fantastic adventures - but this time with NO Captain Red to spoil things. Well that's what we thought...

We could not have imagined what was in store for us, or how dangerous our summer holiday was going to be...

Chapter 3

Takootu Time

"Greetings, family Smith!" smiled Takootu, shaking our hands warmly. "It is being so wonderful to be seeing you all again - welcome back!"

We had just flown into Bora Bora, a beautiful island in the middle of the South Pacific, famous for its long sandy beaches, volcanoes and palm trees. No teachers or spelling tests to be seen for thousands of miles...

Takootu looked almost exactly the same as before. His jet black hair had a few extra flecks of grey running through it now, but he still stood just as tall and strong. His dark skin was scattered with an amazing assortment of extraordinary tattoos and his eyes and smile were brighter than ever. It was so special to see him again.

"Come, I have some very important persons for you to meet."

Takootu led us towards his old sailing boat, the *Captain Cook*, which was moored at the end of the harbour. As we approached it, four young people jumped down from the deck excitedly.

Two of them looked similar in age to me and Jana and the other two looked a few years older. They all had jet black hair and big brown eyes just like Takootu. They were dressed in shorts and T-shirts similar to us, but their T-shirts looked much more special, with bright colourful images of Polynesia printed on the front.

"These is my children, family Smith," beamed Takootu, proudly. "I is very sorry that I did not get time to show them to you last visit. Their names is Mareva, Tametoa, Nino and Rai. Nino and Rai is twins. Nino is youngest..."

"Only by ten tiny minutes," cried Nino, with a cheeky smile across his face. "But SHE never lets me forget it!"

We all laughed.

"Neither does Jana!" I replied, enthusiastically. "And she's just 11 minutes older…"

"You're a younger twin too!?" gasped Nino, looking ecstatic. "At last - someone who can understand me!"

Nino grinned from ear-to-ear and gave me a spontaneous high five. At that moment I knew that he and I were going to be extremely good friends.

"Mareva is my eldest one," continued Takootu, eagerly. "She now 16 and she is speaking the very good English - almost as good as Takootu."

Takootu chuckled, he knew his English was far from perfect, but at least we could always understand him.

As Takootu introduced us, the children greeted us warmly and placed bright rings of yellow flowers around our necks.

"We are delighted to meet you." said Mareva, smiling sweetly, like a Polynesian princess. "We are so grateful for your bravery in winning back the Lost Treasure of Zeo. We will always be in your debt. Welcome to French Polynesia – the Kingdom of Zeo!"

Suddenly, I started to feel quite important. It was a strange feeling, I'd never felt quite like it before. It was a bit like when you get a certificate in assembly in front of the whole school, but a zillion times better!

"You liking new *Captain Cook*?" asked Takootu, as they helped to take on our luggage. "My children is saying it looked old, so they is helping me to paint it. We choose colours of the Polynesian flag - red, orange and blue. You like?"

"Yes," we all replied, enthusiastically.

It was amazing what a lick of paint could do - it was totally transformed, although I could tell from Mum's expression that she still wasn't feeling confident about its sea worthiness. Soon we were all aboard and on our way. I was starting to feel very excited …

It wouldn't be long now 'til I got to see Minoo.

Chapter 4

Special Children

It was midday now and although the sun was dazzling our eyes, the view from the *Captain Cook* was breathtaking. We could see green emerald islands in the distance and dolphins jumping happily out at sea. It felt like we were in a sunshine paradise.

Takootu told us all about the things they had been doing on Radimatu in preparation for the grand opening of the Museum. It sounded like at school when we were opening the new sports hall, but even worse. Poor Takootu sounded tired.

"So many things to do, very busy," he smiled. "I could not be doing all things without my wonderful children. Always helping me and Zeo. They is being very special to me. They is good children – MOST of time!"

"Not good ALL the time, Papa!?" joked Nino, posing playfully like a saint.

"Definitely not you, Nino!" smiled Mareva, tickling him until he broke out in a fit of giggles.

Takootu smiled.

"Always willing to help? That's just like our two," grinned Mum, giving me a big wink. "We only ever have to ask once, isn't that right, Dad?"

Dad looked surprised, and then smirked. "We wish!"

"Aren't we special children too?" asked Jana, sounding a little jealous.

"Of course you are, precious." comforted Mum, giving Jana a big cuddle. "Very special."

The breeze was fresh as our boat pitched up and down in the turquoise blue water. Soon we would be at Zeo. Soon I would be with Minoo…

Takootu stood at the helm and allowed us turns to steer

the *Captain Cook*, by turning the large timber wheel. It was such great fun. Takootu asked us lots of questions about our year back in England, then after a while he started to tell us more about his children. He seemed extremely proud of them.

"Zeo is giving them all different talents," he explained excitedly. "Tametoa is Champion canoer and swimmer on our island."

"Only 'cause I let him win!" smirked Nino, cheekily.

"Sure you did Nino," replied Rai, raising her eyes to the heavens. "Tametoa won the 'Radimatu Va'a Island Race' for the second time this April – that's five times around our island in a canoe and three times around swimming!"

"Wow!" I cried, excitedly. "That's some going – awesome."

"I feel exhausted just thinking about it," laughed Dad. "What a fantastic achievement."

"Rai prefers the swimming under the water," continued

Takootu, proudly. "She is Champion Diver in her year, but she is having another special talent too. Sometimes she is knowing things before they actually is happening. Especially dangerous things."

"Really?" cried Jana, excitedly. "Like a sixth sense - how special. That would come in very handy at night when my sneaky brother has hidden a creepy-crawly spider in my bed."

We all laughed together in the glorious sunshine. We were certainly finding out a lot about our new friends. Suddenly I noticed that Nino wasn't looking as happy as the rest of us. He coughed loudly and waited, as though he was feeling a bit left out.

"Sorry Nino," continued Takootu, as the *Captain Cook* surged forward, "I is coming to you next. Nino is the fastest ..."

"Talker!" interrupted Tametoa, mischievously. "He never shuts up!"

We all laughed - including Nino, who didn't seem to mind at all.

"It is being true." smiled Takootu. "Nino does like the talking lots and I is very sure if there is being a chatter-box champion on our island – Nino is winning it easily. But he is also the Radimatu Champion sprinter in his year – he goes as fast as the Mata'i which blows from the east."

"Thanks Papa," – shouted Nino, playfully. "You're pretty quick too… for an old man!"

"Cheeky, Nino," smiled Takootu affectionately. "Always the joker!"

"Jay is a fast runner too," quipped Dad. "Especially when it's his turn to wash up!"

I smirked and stuck my tongue out playfully. Takootu chuckled and looked ahead, where we could see a multitude of small islands in the distance.

"What about Mareva, Takootu?" asked Jana, eagerly. "Tell us about Mareva…"

Takootu paused and looked admiringly towards her.

"Mareva is one of the fiercest fighters in Radimatu,"

replied Takootu, bursting with pride. "She is winning the young Radi warrior award for the third year running."

"Yeah, don't mess with my big sis!" joked Nino, swishing his Rodu through the air. "She's lethal!"

Mareva smiled and looked a little self conscious.

"But that is not all," continued Takootu, looking suddenly quite upset. "Mareva is having the biggest heart in Polynesia. Since we lost their Mama, Mareva is having to do lots more things in house – caring for us all … caring for Mama too when she is being so unwell. Always happy and smiling. She is being example for us all."

This was SAD. I wondered why Takootu had never mentioned his wife before. Now I understood why. How heartbreaking for them all.

"Land ahoy!" cried Tametoa, excitedly from the front of the boat. "Island Zeo!"

I peered eagerly through Grandad's telescope …

It WAS Island Zeo, and it looked just as I remembered…

Chapter 5

Return to Zeo

Butterflies were flying around in my tummy, as I raced up the beach towards our old tree house. Happy memories from the year before flooded through my head – it felt so good to be back.

"Minoo!" I shouted excitedly, arriving at our tree house. "It's me. We're here. We're HOME!"

There was no reply. No friendly face or cheeky chattering from the trees. I felt slightly empty and disappointed, but really I was being silly. How could I expect Minoo to know we were here after all this time?

I ran up and down the long sandy beach calling his name and gazing high up into the emerald green canopy, but still there was no sign of him. I started to feel a bit sick and scared. What if something had happened to him? What if he had forgotten all about me and couldn't even remember who I was?

The sun felt hot on my back as I continued searching. Then after a minute or so the others arrived and started to join in. Soon, everyone was calling for him.

"Minoo!" shouted Nino, looking high up in the palm trees.

"Minoo!" shouted Rai, looking over towards the lagoon.

But STILL there was no sign of him …

"We'll find him, Jay," said Mum, who could tell I was getting worried.

"Yes, not you worry Jay," smiled Takootu reassuringly, as he broke open a large coconut on the rocks.

"Minoo is being here soon. Trust Takootu. He probably up that tree watching. Be still everyone. Minoo will come to us..."

We all stood still for a few moments and listened

carefully. We could hear the waves tumbling onto the shore, insects buzzing in and out of colourful exotic flowers and green and red parrots squawking noisily.

Takootu put his finger to his ear.

"Listen - I is hearing something ..."

Suddenly there was a rustling in the branches above us and I heard a familiar chattering sound ...

Then before I knew it, a cheeky white-faced monkey swung out of the tree and landed right in front of us. It was MINOO!

He looked at me quizzically, as though he was just checking it really was me. Then he leapt up into my arms and straight onto my head! I wrestled him off playfully and threw him high up into the air - like I always did - remembering to catch him of course.

The others all laughed and Takootu smiled warmly. "I tell you young Jay not worry - Minoo is never forgetting you. You special to him, like my children is special to me."

"And like you are special to us." added Mum, hastily, before Jana had time to ask.

Takootu leant over and gave Minoo some coconut to eat, which he eagerly accepted. As we looked up, we noticed many more monkeys jumping and chattering, parrots squawking and birds tweeting. It was as though they were all welcoming our return to Island Zeo. It felt so special to be back, but especially to be back with Minoo and Takootu.

Sadly, Takootu had to leave us early.

"Goodbye family Smith. Takootu is going now. Things to do. I is returning later. My family is looking after you. Enjoy island Zeo."

"Thanks Takootu - we will!" I replied, excitedly.

Takootu said a few things to Mareva in Tahitian and then sailed away on the *Captain Cook*, waving cheerfully from the helm.

We still had most of the day left and I was determined to make up for lost time with Minoo, but little did I know what surprises were in store for us …

Chapter 6

Seeing RED

"Let's all play with Minoo," I shouted to the others excitedly. "We can show you our island and we might even find some more treasure!"

Jana raised her eyebrows and scoffed. "Please excuse my crazy brother - he's got TREASURE on the brain!"

The others all laughed.

"We are very pleased he has," replied Mareva cheerfully. "Or he might not have found the Lost Treasure of Zeo for us."

The others smiled and laughed again. It was strange having someone on my side for a change. I liked it.

First we showed them the small thistle-like plants that grew all over our island and warned them NEVER to fall in them.

"I can see why you called it 'Prickly-PONG'…"
laughed Nino. "It STINKS!"

"It's painful too," I replied. "Especially if you land in it
– like I did!"

"Thanks for the warning," smiled Mareva. "We will
definitely keep away."

We all played tig down on the beach to start. Nino was
like lightning – no one could catch him, except Minoo.

"Can't we play something else?" moaned Jana. "I'm
always IT."

Next we played 'Coconut Catch'. Nino and Rai loved
it, especially when Minoo's monkey friends joined in
too. Unfortunately, it got a little bit out of hand and a
large coconut caught poor Rai on the back of her head.

"Your sixth sense didn't help you this time," joked
Nino, giving her some of his drink.

"Don't worry, Rai," I said to her, "I know something that will help the pain."

But before I knew it, Minoo appeared with some leavesof the little yellow plant we had named 'Prickly-Gone'. I rubbed the leaves gently against Rai's head like Minoo had shown me last year.

"Better?" I asked.

"Much," smiled Rai, looking surprised. "The pain has completely gone!"

"Clever plant!" cried Mareva.

"Clever Minoo, too!" Rai added cheerfully.

Minoo looked extremely pleased with himself. He stood on his head and started to pull some VERY silly faces.

Suddenly there was a large cry and Nino crashed out of a giant palm tree right on top of a HUGE patch of Prickly-Pong. He cried out in agony and started to shout words in his own language. (Pity I don't speak Tahitian as I'm pretty certain some of them were quite rude.)

"Poor, Nino," comforted Jana.

"SILLY, Nino!" joked Tametoa. "For thinking he is a monkey like Minoo."

We couldn't help laughing, even though Nino was still in some distress.

"Stay still, Nino," ordered Jana. "We know something that will take away the pain..."

Minoo appeared again with some more of his magic healing plant, and it wasn't long before Nino was smiling and joking again. We were all feeling tired and hot, so we took drinks of cool water from the island spring and watched the waves crashing on the shore.

"Ready for more exploring?" asked Jana. "We could walk right up to the top of the cliff where there is a lovely view."

"Yes - last one up is a wobbly jelly fish," I cried, as I started to sprint up the steep path. "Follow me!"

Within a few minutes we were all at the top of 'High Rock' and Jana (the jelly fish) was right, the views were amazing.

We could see for miles, right across Polynesia, island upon island glistening in the bright sunshine.

"There's our home!" shouted Nino, excitedly, who was the first to the top with me.

"Yes, it's very close to you here on Zeo," smiled Mareva.

"So close I could swim it," joked Tametoa.

Well I think he was joking.

While everyone was admiring the spectacular views, I suddenly noticed a ship to the north, very close to Prickly-Pong Island, which had been our first home last year. Nino had noticed it too.

"Look!" he cried. "It looks like one of those old-fashioned galleons we have pictures of in the museum."

Nino was right. It was one of those old-fashioned ships. One that looked strangely familiar to me. I reached for grandad's telescope, (which I always carried on a cord around my neck), and inspected it more closely...

It was no ordinary schooner – it looked identical to a

ship we knew only too well from our adventures last year...

Captain Red's galleon - the *Golden Age*...!

A shudder went down my spine. What on earth was HE doing HERE?

"Jana! Jana!" I cried, nervously, thrusting the telescope towards her. "Look, quickly - it's Red's ship! Look!"

Jana glared at me and smiled. "Yeah, yeah – good one, Jay. I'm not falling for another of your stupid jokes."

"Captain Red?" inquired Nino looking alarmed. "The one who tried to steal Zeo's Treasure?"

"Yes him," I replied, urgently. "I'm not joking, Jana - it's Red's ship! Please, look – before he goes out of view…"

"Go on then, but if you're teasing me I'll push you right off this cliff!"

Jana grabbed the telescope and peered out towards Prickly-Pong Island.

"Can't see a thing, Jay." she hissed, raising the telescope in the air as though she was about to bash me with it. "I knew it was a tease."

"It wasn't a tease, honest it wasn't. It was Red's ship – I'm sure it was!"

"There WAS a ship out there," said Nino. "I saw it too."

"Yes, OK there was a ship, I believe there was a ship, but it could have been ANY old ship," sighed Jana, impatiently. "Please excuse my younger brother - like I said before, he's got pirates and treasure on the brain!"

The others laughed, but I didn't see the funny side.

"I think your brother is telling the truth," said Mareva, sounding more concerned. "I'm sure he would not make up stories to us."

"Not on purpose perhaps, Mareva" replied Jana, annoyingly. "But Jay thinks about Captain Red all the time – he even has dreams about him – so I'm not surprised that the first day we are here in Polynesia he thinks he's seen him. That's all."

"Well I hope that you are right, Jana." said Mareva, looking slightly uneasy. "We certainly don't want Captain Red and his pirates spoiling the opening tomorrow…"

As we ran back down the path towards camp, I started to feel really agitated, but not just because Jana didn't believe me – I was SCARED!

If that WAS Captain Red's galleon - which I was 99 per cent certain it was - what on earth was he doing HERE?

Was he planning to do something despicable and dastardly? Was he plotting to steal back the treasure…?

Terrifying thoughts raced through my brain. I would tell Takootu immediately he returned. I'm sure he would want to know and what's more, I'm sure he would believe me.

Chapter 7

Bottles of Rum

Takootu wasn't due back for a while still, so after a quick lunch we decided to play hide and seek. At least it would help to take my mind off things. We had to explain the rules to the others first, as they had never played it before.

"Count to a hundred," I shouted back to Jana. "And remember - NO peeping!"

Mareva and Nino were in my team and Minoo of course. We raced into the lush green undergrowth, dodging in and out of huge patches of Prickly-Pong as we went.

"They'll never find us," I whispered excitedly. "I know a great place!"

We headed up a steep hill towards Coconut Cliff, where Minoo and I had often played last year.

After a few minutes, Minoo started making strange noises and started pulling on my hand annoyingly.

"What's the matter with you?" I inquired.

Minoo kept on pulling.

"I think he wants us to follow him," said Mareva.

"Maybe he has a surprise hiding place to show us," replied Nino excitedly. "Follow that monkey!"

Minoo led us up through a huge clump of coconut palms and up high towards the top of the hill.

"I can hear them coming behind us," whispered Mareva, urgently.

"Quick, Minoo!" I cried. "We need to hide now or they'll see us…"

Minoo started chattering excitedly and pointed towards a large round rock just ahead of us. He bounded forward, jumped up onto the boulder - then COMPLETELY disappeared…

We sprinted up to see where he had got to and could just make out a small opening in the ground. It looked like a cave.

"Quick," I whispered to the others. "In here!"

We crept down into the opening, as quickly as we could and Minoo was there waiting for us.

It WAS a cave! There wasn't much light, but we could just about make out the walls. It was pleasantly cool, but there was a yucky smell of damp.

"Quiet!" I whispered to everyone. "They're CLOSE! Hopefully they won't notice the opening…"

We could hear them talking just outside. Jana was giving out instructions to the others.

"We're coming to get you LOSERS!!" she shouted. "We know where you are…"

Our hearts sank in disappointment. Surely, they hadn't seen us? We just hoped she was bluffing…

After a few agonizing seconds the voices outside started to become quieter and quieter, until we could hear them no more.

"We DID it," I whispered quietly. "Well done everyone. What a brilliant hiding place, Minoo!"

Normally Minoo would have let out one of his squeals of delight or stood on his head and pulled silly faces, but he didn't seem happy at all. He tugged on my arm again and disappeared into the gloom of the cave.

As our eyes got accustomed to the dim light, it soon became clear why Minoo had brought us here. It looked like people had been using the cave as a DEN! There were blankets in one corner and the remains of a fire near the entrance. The others needed to see this, so I called them in straight away.

"No wonder, we didn't see you," cried Jana, squinting in the dim light. "What a brilliant hiding place."

"Yes, that's why the visitors must have chosen it," replied Nino excitedly, pointing out the blankets in the corner.

Before Jana and the others had time to react, Minoo appeared from the darkness holding up a bottle and chattering animatedly.

"Looks like we've had some strangers visiting our island while we've been away," I exclaimed, anxiously. "That's why Minoo wanted to bring us here!"

"Strangers who likes drinking rum!" cried Tametoa, inspecting the bottle more closely.

"Strangers who like drinking LOTS of rum!" exclaimed Nino excitedly, holding up two more bottles in his hand. "There must be another ten empty bottles over there at least."

All of a sudden I started to feel anxious.

"PIRATES like drinking rum…" I murmured slowly.

"Not pirates AGAIN, Jay!" groaned Jana.

"I saw a brilliant pirate movie last week," continued Nino excitedly, pretending to drink from the bottles. "Yo, ho, ho and a bottle of rum…"

The others started to laugh at Nino who continued buffooning around, but I didn't feel like joining in this time. The possibility that the strangers who had stayed here were PIRATES sent a shiver down my spine.

I continued searching around for more clues. Suddenly my attention was taken by Minoo who was jumping up and down excitedly by the fire. I ran over to investigate.

Close to the ashes, I noticed a piece of screwed up paper - singed at the edges. I picked it up eagerly and examined it in the dim light. All I could make out was that it was some sort of map.

My heart missed a beat...

Not ANOTHER treasure map, I thought…

Chapter 8

The Map

I moved quickly over towards the entrance of the cave, where a shaft of bright sunlight was streaming through and studied it more closely. It looked like the outline of an island and there was a big 'X' drawn, near the coast. There was some writing on it too, but it was difficult to make out what it said.

"Look!" I shouted to the others, excitedly. "I think I might have found a map - a TREASURE map…"

"Pirates and Treasure?" scoffed Jana, rolling her eyes. "Is that really ALL you ever think about, Jay?"

The others rushed over eagerly and examined the map.

"Radimatu," cried Nino, excitedly. "It's our island!"

The others agreed unanimously. They all looked stunned.

"Lost treasure on our island?" cheered Rai. "How exciting!"

"And we are going there later today!" cheered Jana.

"NO!" said Mareva, suddenly looking extremely troubled by something. "This is not good."

She spoke to Tametoa in Tahitian for a few moments, and then started to look more closely at the map again. Both of them suddenly looked extremely disturbed.

"The persons who drew this map have a very big interest in our little island and especially in our new Museum!" said Mareva, anxiously.

"The X on this map is in the exact location of our new Museum – where Zeo's Treasure is kept." added Tametoa, uneasily.

"And the writing on the map… We think it's a date. We think it reads, August 1st…" added Mareva, looking extremely alarmed.

I inspected the writing again closely. They were right. It did look like a date...... AUG 1.

"That's tomorrow!" Jana exclaimed. "It's the day of the opening. Why would someone draw such a map and write on a date unless, unless...

"They are planning to steal Zeo's Treasure!" I blurted out loudly.

Mareva and Tametoa didn't reply, but we could tell by their silence that THAT was what they were thinking too. At that moment, Minoo appeared again holding up what looked like a gentleman's sash. I recognised it instantly – it looked like Captain Red's!

"Are you sure, Jay?" asked Jana, hesitantly. "It does look very similar to the one he wears around his waist, but it could just be a coincidence ..?"

"It could be," I replied, doubtfully – hoping that Jana might be right, but feeling in my bones that she wasn't.

"Use your sixth sense, Rai!" cried Nino, urgently, thrusting the red sash into her hands.

Rai took the sash suspiciously and closed her eyes as though she was going deep into a kind of trance. After a few seconds (which seemed like years) she nodded unhappily.

"If my senses are right - it's his..."

"Curse him!" cried Tametoa, grabbing the sash violently and trying to rip it into pieces.

"Sorry, Jay," said Jana, looking upset. "You were right to have pirates on your mind. This is the worst. I'm scared – really scared! I bet it really was Captain Red's galleon that you saw earlier today."

It all started to make sense. The Captain and his pirates must have used this cave for a hideout. From Island Zeo they could easily see over to Radimatu and plan an attack. The question was what were we going to do about it now? How could we stop them?

"Do not worry Jay and Jana – we will be ready for any pirates IF they come," cried Tametoa, courageously. "And especially if it is that cowardly criminal Captain Red!"

"Yes, please do not worry," said Mareva calmly. "When we tell Papa he will know what to do."

Chapter 9

Troubled Takootu

As soon as Takootu returned later that afternoon in the *Captain Cook*, we broke the bad news. Mareva did most of the talking and when she showed him the burnt piece of map, his expression turned instantly to concern.

"You is doing very well, Jay." said Takootu, calmly. "Thank you for discovering map – this is being very important to my island and people."

"Is everything going to be all right at the opening?" asked Jana, nervously.

"Yes young Jana, of course," replied Takootu. "Everything is being fine. Thanks to Minoo and your clever discovery we will be ready for Captain Red and his pirates, if they is coming – do not fear!"

As Takootu said these words, Mareva and Tametoa raised their Rodu above their heads and let out a loud Radi battle cry.

"Itoito! Itoito!"

"Zeo will give us courage!" cried Mareva, assuredly, as Rai and Nino joined in the battle cry too.

I hoped and prayed that Takootu was right, but my mind kept flashing back to the last time we crossed swords with Captain Red - when we were all lucky to survive. I suddenly started to feel quite sick inside. I wasn't the only one thinking about Captain Red. Suddenly Mum and Dad started to have one of their 'boring' conversations about how risky it all sounded.

"Could it be very dangerous, Takootu?" inquired Mum, her voice quivering slightly. "Will the children be safe?"

Takootu walked over to Mum and Dad and sat down next to them reassuringly.

"I am sorry Mr and Mrs Smith - yes, it could be being

dangerous. I cannot be saying it won't. You will have to be deciding the best thing to be done for your family. If you is preferring to stay here at Zeo, I am completely understanding…"

"No, Mum," I shouted, disappointedly. "No way. We want go with Takootu and his family to help!"

"But it could be very dangerous," said Dad, firmly.

"I is letting you discuss matter in private, as family." continued Takootu. "Come children, we get boat ready."

Things didn't look good. Mum and Dad's minds seemed made up. We were going to be grounded and banned from going with Takootu. Banned from opening the Museum - our special day was going up in smoke. But then something amazing happened. Jana started to use her persuasive skills…

"Staying here at Zeo could be even more dangerous," pleaded Jana. "What if the pirates come back to do more scheming in their cave – we'll be here ALL alone!"

Mum's face suddenly went very pale. She could remember how merciless Captain Red could be. Dad didn't look too happy either.

"Jana is right," said Dad. "We will be safer if we go with Takootu".

I almost couldn't believe it. My clever twin sister had come to the rescue in the nick of time. Dad went to let Takootu know their decision, and in a matter of minutes we had set sail to Radimatu - with Minoo on board as my very own special guest!

Chapter 10

Look Out!

Everyone was a little quiet on board as we started to travel the relatively short distance across the sea to Radimatu. I could only imagine how Takootu and his family were feeling, but I knew it wouldn't be good. Takootu asked us all to keep a close look out on the horizon for any strange vessels. By that, we all knew what he meant - PIRATE SHIPS!

I took out grandad's old telescope (the one Takootu had used to battle off Captain Red last summer) and started to gaze into the distance...

"Anything unusual you is seeing – just shout," Takootu reminded us all urgently.

All I could see was blue ocean and island upon island -

nothing else.

Minoo soon found his sailing feet and within a matter of minutes he was at the top of the mast with an even better view than mine.

"Clever, Minoo," smiled, Rai. "Tell us if you spot anything."

Minoo pulled a funny face and started chattering to himself. After a while, Nino started to show us some of his Radi fighting moves to take out Captain Red.

"He won't stand a chance, against me!" cried Nino, as he swung his Rodu skillfully and confidently through the air.

Nino's play acting would normally have brought smiles and laughter to us all, but not at this moment. Suddenly things felt a lot more serious. Today, he was only play-fighting, but tomorrow it might be for real…

"Keep eyes open please," reminded Takootu cheerfully, as he surveyed the horizon watchfully.

All of a sudden we were alerted by a loud squeaking

sound coming from Minoo. We all looked out to sea apprehensively. We were expecting to catch a glimpse of the callous, coldblooded Captain Red and his cowardly crew, but we all got an unexpected surprise.

Out in the ocean came a small fleet of Radi, in their wonderfully decorated canoes. The tattooed Radi warriors came alongside and exchanged friendly greetings with us all. Then Takootu started to talk to them in Tahitian in a very sombre tone, and we all guessed what he was telling them.

The Radi suddenly looked extremely angry and upset, but Takootu kept talking to them in a calm fatherly voice. He sounded like he was giving them important instructions of what to do. After this brief exchange, the Radi warriors waved farewell to us all, then sailed off speedily, as though their lives depended on it.

"Itoito! Itoito!" shouted Mareva, Nino and Rai, raising their Rodu above their heads once more.

"The Radi warriors will take care of Captain Red and his cowardly pirates if they dare to come..!" cried

Tametoa defiantly, joining in the chant.

I prayed Tametoa was right…

Chapter 11

Sacred Radimatu

It wasn't long before we were close to the shores of Radimatu and for a minute or two all thoughts of Captain Red went right out of our heads. Mareva started to point out various points of interest to us, and she sounded like she was a professional tour guide.

"There is Mount Tamoni – where tiare apetahi grows - the rarest plant in the world!"

"How spectacular," cried Mum. "It looks so majestic!"

"It's actually a volcano!" smirked Nino, playfully.

Mum suddenly looked alarmed, until Mareva reassured her it hadn't erupted for hundreds of years.

"There is the Sacred Forest of Zeo, where the wood for

all the Rodu come from." continued Mareva.

"The trees look so extraordinary," remarked Dad,
admiringly.

"Yes Mr Smith," replied Takootu, enthusiastically.
"They say Sacred Forest is being six hundred years old
or more. Zeo's gift to us."

Their island looked so beautiful. It reminded me of
Gigantuki Island (before it got destroyed by the giant
Prickly-Pong) but it was much, much bigger. We could
see mountains, magnificent cliffs, cascading waterfalls,
and a huge emerald green forest of coconut palms
shimmering in the late afternoon sunshine. It was
breathtaking.

I could see why Takootu and his people had lived here
for so many years and why it was called 'Sacred'
Radimatu. It looked like it had been created by a higher
power.

"Dolphins!" cried Jana, suddenly pointing excitedly.

She was right. Just a few metres from the boat, three

blue dolphins were swimming alongside the *Captain Cook*.

"How wonderful!" cried Mum.

"AMAZING!" agreed Jana, eagerly.

The dolphins came right up to the edge of the boat and one of them seemed particularly friendly, jumping up out of the water as if it was talking to us.

"Meet Poe," beamed Rai, cheerfully. "She is my best friend, like Minoo is to you."

"The one with the black nose is my Puati," added Mareva. "She is the highest jumper."

"Oh no she isn't!" smiled Rai, confidently. "Poe can out-jump them all."

"I'll settle it!" cried Nino. "Watch this…"

He picked up a small piece of shrimp from a bucket by the rail and hurled it high into the air. Almost instantly, all three dolphins soared speedily out of the turquoise blue ocean spinning acrobatically towards their prize.

"Wow!" cried, Jana, excitedly. "It's like watching one of those 'Marine-World' TV shows. They look incredible!"

Nino and Tametoa kept throwing more shrimp into the air and the dolphins kept leaping high into the sky. It soon became clear who the winner was.

"OK, Rai. You win!" winked Mareva. "Poe is definitely the highest jumper, but Puati is still the deepest diver."

We all laughed and then applauded, but the dolphins weren't finished yet. Within seconds, six more appeared along the other side of our boat, flying and leaping over the waves and spiralling into the sky.

It was magical. A sight we will never forget. It felt as though we were being escorted into shore by our very own shoal of dolphins.

Chapter 12

Pearl Problems

As we got closer to shore, we started to see intricate beds of coral with bright colourful fish darting in all directions. There were giant turtles too.

"Look!" exclaimed, Rai, pointing towards a multi-coloured part of the reef. "That's where Mareva and I work."

"Yes, this is where we dive for pearls most afternoons," explained Mareva, waving to some of her friends as we passed.

Mareva explained that the pearls came from small creatures called oysters that live in the coral, with hundreds of other fish and sea creatures.

"How exciting," beamed Jana. "Real pearls! You're a lot braver than me diving down THAT far."

"We couldn't do it without help from our dolphin family, could we Mareva?" smiled Rai.

"No we couldn't," agreed, Mareva enthusiastically. "They look after us every day. They dive down with us on the coral beds and help us back to the surface with our catch. Poe saved Rai's life last year when she bumped her head on a huge rock and fell unconscious – Poe raised the alarm and helped bring her back to the surface. They are our very special friends and now they are your special friends too."

"It's our job most days after school," said Rai proudly, waving to more of her people who were dotted all about the reef. "We find many pearls and we give them to the craft people who make beautiful jewellery. Some items we keep for our people, but most are taken to Paris and other French cities."

"Papa says too many are being taken to Paris," added Mareva, looking quite frustrated. "Soon there won't be any for anyone…"

"Mareva is right," added Takootu, looking upset. "Remember what I is telling you the first day we meet? *You look after island and island is looking after you…*"

Mareva explained that Radimatu, like most islands in the area, was a French colony and was controlled by France.

"We should be allowed to do what we want – not what the French government tells us."   shouted Tametoa, angrily. "This is land of Zeo - Polynesia not Paris!"

Although it was Tametoa speaking I got the feeling that all the others felt the same, especially Takootu and Mareva.

"The more they is wanting us to fish," said Takootu looking quite troubled, "the more the coral getting damaged. Soon there is being no coral. No place for oysters and fish to live. Then there is being no pearls and no fish for us to catch!"

"That's crazy!" shouted Jana, furiously. "Don't governments realise what is happening? It's a disgrace!"

Since last year, when our beautiful Gigantuki island had been destroyed by the giant Prickly-Pong, we had all started taking a keen interest in environmental issues. But Jana was by far the most passionate.

"At Conservation Club, we learnt that coral reefs are dying all over the world from pollution, over-fishing and higher temperatures." continued Jana, heatedly "We shouldn't let it happen - it's criminal!"

"You is right, young Jana." replied Takootu, solemnly. "I wish people in power is having your youthful wisdom and common sense."

Takootu was looking uneasy and I could totally

understand why. He and his people had enough concerns already without Captain Red plotting to steal their treasure. It just wasn't fair.

Chapter 13

Polynesian Welcome

As we got closer to shore, we started to see more and more people smiling and waving.

"You are very popular, Chief Takootu," I said, "Look at all your people."

Takootu laughed and beamed a big smile.

"They is waving and smiling at you - not me. They is so thankful for what you all did for them. You is famous, like royal family now…"

Suddenly, l started to feel quite special – and I'm sure the others did too. There were island people everywhere and they were all waving and welcoming us. They were on the beach, in the fruit fields, on the high cliff top and some were even waving from the top of huge palm trees.

"You is all celebrities," smiled Takootu. "They is all wanting to meet you and shake your hands."

Suddenly we reaslised that if they were waving at US, then we ought to be waving back. So that's what we did. We waved at everyone we could see. The fishermen in their boats, the Radi warriors in their canoes, the children and families lining the shore – everyone.

Mareva explained that all the islanders had been given a two-day holiday in honour of our visit to open the Museum. It also coincided with their special religious day to honour their Tahitian god Zeo.

"You think this is a lot of people?" joked Nino. "Just you wait until tomorrow!"

The island people seemed so humble, friendly and caring; I couldn't bear to think of how sad they would feel if Captain Red DID steal their treasure from them. The thought that the despicable Captain had the nerve and skullduggery to be plotting to take their treasure, made by blood boil! It was Zeo's Treasure and it belonged to Takootu and his wonderful island people.

I vowed I would do anything I could to help them, and I knew Minoo and Jana would help out too. I just hoped there was something we could do to prevent it. At least the Radi warriors would be ready for them, if they dared to make an attack.

Chapter 14

Wonderful Radimatu

Takootu steered the boat skillfully into the small timber-built harbour, and as he did he looked over to us with a glint in his eye.

"Look up there, Jay and Jana! Takootu is having a little surprise for you both."

We peered into the crowd of people who had gathered high up on the harbour wall and there, standing right at the front, were two very familiar faces…

It was Grandma and Grandad! They were dressed in

bright summery clothes, but we recognised them instantly. We were both completely stunned.

"You didn't think I was going to miss another chance of an adventure did you, young man?" cried Grandad excitedly, helping us up with our luggage.

"I know we're old, but we're not so old that we can't travel on a plane." beamed Grandma, giving us one of her legendary big hugs. "Besides, we didn't want to miss your special moment!"

I glanced over to Mum and Dad, and I could see them smirking like a pair of naughty school kids. They had known all along. What a BRILLIANT surprise. Grandma and Grandad would be staying for the opening and then flying off for a holiday in Hawaii.

"Mareva is looking after you now, family Smith." said Takootu, briskly. "I is having important jobs to do. Please you excuse me. But I is seeing you at dinner. Enjoy your tour! You is special guests on our island..."

The next few hours went by like a whirlwind. We were all treated like VIP's, to a lightning quick guided tour around all the top sights of Radimatu. There were wonderful waterfalls running down from the mountains and farms full of exotic fruits and flowers.

"What's that gorgeous sweet smell?" asked Mum, breathing in deeply.

"It's vanilla," smiled, Mareva. "We grow it all over the island. Lovely isn't it?"

The whole island was spectacular and there was a real carnival atmosphere in the main town. Many of the villagers were dressed in traditional Tahitian costumes which looked amazing.

"What beautiful outfits," cried, Grandma admiringly. "Those headdresses are simply stunning!"

"So colourful," agreed Mum.

"You will all be wearing one of your own outfits tomorrow," replied Rai, excitedly. "We've even got one for Minoo!"

Mareva explained that the islanders had made us all items of traditional dress that we could wear to the opening if we wanted to or just keep them as a souvenir.

"How thoughtful and special," said Grandma "I've always wanted to wear a Tahitian grass skirt."

"Maybe I could have a special tattoo done too?" I asked, hopefully. "Like yours Tametoa?"

Tametoa had a striking black tattoo on his right forearm which looked really cool.

"You have to be at least fifteen to get one of those," sighed Nino, glumly.

"I'm definitely old enough to have one then," smiled Grandad, "Maybe I will surprise you all!"

We all laughed and continued on our visit. The people were so friendly and welcoming. As we walked around, they kept coming up to us and presenting us with small hand-made presents and colourful rings of flowers to put on our heads or around our necks.

"What a beautiful, necklace!" beamed Jana. "Thank you so much."

"It's made from local shells," explained Rai.

"Might smell a bit fishy!" joked Nino.

"Nonsense, Nino," smiled Mareva. "It looks and smells wonderful!"

We all laughed again.

The next stop was the open market and WOW - was it spectacular. There were all sorts of things for sale. There were exotic fruits and vegetables and fish of all sizes and colours.

"All freshly caught or picked today," said Mareva, passing us all some pineapple to try.

"Delicious!" cried Jana.

Just at that minute we noticed Minoo on the roof of the fruit store happily munching his way through a huge bunch of grapes.

"Naughty Minoo!" I shouted, feeling a little embarrassed. "You haven't paid for those - put them down."

"Don't worry, Jay." replied Mareva, affectionately. "He deserves something nice after his brilliant detective work. I'll treat him."

The lady at the store wouldn't take any money and gave Minoo even more grapes to eat, free of charge. Minoo looked extremely pleased with himself and continued chomping contentedly. We all smiled and carried on exploring the market.

In the next section, there was an incredible range of craft stores. Colourful blankets called tifaifai; painted sarongs called pareus; hand-carved musical instruments and beautiful coral and shell jewellery.

"This is where I got my new canoe," added Nino, pointing to the boat store. "I will take you out in it later."

"Awesome!" I replied eagerly.

"I wish I could stay for a whole month – not just a few days," cried Grandma, excitedly. "It's so wonderful!"

Grandma was right – it was a wonderful island – made even more wonderful by the people.

"Look at all those Rodu," cried Grandad, looking very impressed. "There must be more than a hundred."

"All handmade from Forest Zeo," added Tametoa, proudly.

Tametoa and Nino gave Grandad a quick demonstration of how to use the Rodu – just like we had done at school for 'Show and Tell'. He loved it.

"I think I need to buy one of these to protect myself from NINO!" joked Grandad, playfully. "He is positively dangerous!"

We all laughed and Nino held up his Rodu above his head like he had just won the Radimatu championship.

"Nobody dares to mess with NINO!"

Chapter15

Zeo's Treasure

The most exciting part of the tour was when we came to the Museum where the treasure was being kept. The following day we would all be here as special guests for the big opening.

The main entrance looked extremely grand. It was covered in elaborate Polynesian designs similar to the patterns we had seen on the Radi canoes.

"What a fine looking structure," said Dad, who has always fancied himself as a bit of a building expert. "The geometric designs are stunning."

"Thank you," replied Mareva, her face full of pride. "The art work is inspired by Zeo, our sacred Polynesian God, and ancient stories from the past handed down from generation to generation. It has meant a lot of hard work for many of our people, but we are all very pleased with it."

"It's delightful," said Mum.

"Magnificent!" added Grandma, taking a sneaky photo.

"Our people have decorated it with some of the pearls we have caught," smiled Rai, pointing at an image of the sun excitedly.

"They look so beautiful!" marvelled Jana.

"Talking of precious stones," quipped Grandad, eagerly, "Where's this amazing treasure then?"

"In there somewhere..." replied Mareva, secretly.

"Papa has quadrupled the guard," said Tametoa

confidently. "Captain Red will never get to our treasure now. We will be ready for them tomorrow – if they dare come."

"Yes," shouted Nino, swishing the air with his Rodu, excitedly. "We will teach those cowardly pirates a lesson!"

I really hoped Nino and Tametoa were right. The Radi warriors certainly looked very fierce and formidable and there must have been at least thirty of them. Grandma and Grandad suddenly looked very confused, so we told them all about our discovery on Island Zeo.

"Not that Captain Red again…!" roared Grandad, angrily. "I'll give him what for if I ever see him. Wish I'd brought my old army rifle…"

Suddenly one of the guards came over to Mareva and spoke to her quietly. He was tall and muscular and looked like he could take on Captain Red and his pirates single handed. We thought there was a problem, but there wasn't. Atonui was the head guard, and had just asked Mareva if we were interested in a quick peep inside at the treasure. Our reply was prompt and unanimous - we really were being treated like royalty!

"This is a bonus," cried Grandad cheerfully. "What a surprise - Zeo's Treasure…"

Atonui guided us down into a long corridor that looked almost like a tunnel.

"Are these the 'lava tubes'?" inquired Jana, flicking through her local guide book.

"Yes," replied Mareva. "A maze of mysterious tunnels and caves formed from the last volcanic eruption. We have used some of them for the Museum – but it has taken considerable time to strengthen all the sides and ceilings.

"What an ingenious idea," said Dad, looking up impressively at the decorated walls. "So unique."

"Thank you," replied Mareva. "Soon we will have exhibits in several of the renovated caves formed from the larva."

"It says here that the larva's temperature got to 2,200

Fahrenheit!!" cried Jana, nervously.

"WOW" cried Nino, excitedly. "That sounds HOT!"

"Well I hope it doesn't erupt again - this week!" cried Mum, starting to look slightly anxious.

"Definitely NOT tomorrow," smiled Dad.

"Don't worry Mrs Smith," replied Mareva, reassuringly. "It hasn't erupted for over three hundred years!"

We all laughed and carried on down the long corridor, briefly stopping and looking into the room-like spaces on the way which contained various exhibits.

Eventually we came to a massive room almost as big as our school hall. It looked lavish and luxurious. The walls were covered in more elaborate Polynesian designs similar to the ones we had seen outside. At the centre of the room, set up high on what looked like an altar, was the TREASURE!

It looked just like we had remembered it from twelve months ago. The old wooden chest, weathered and worn over the years, with its rusty metal clasp on the side. Minoo pointed and started chattering excitedly, as though he had just seen a long lost friend.

As we drew closer we could see that the chest lay open, with its contents visible for all to see…

"How wonderful!" gasped Grandma.

We all fell silent as we were filled with a sense of awe and beauty.

There were sparkling dark-green emeralds; shimmering white diamonds; gleaming red rubies and glistening yellow pearls. Not to mention, hundreds and hundreds of golden brown Doubloons.

"How spectacular!" gasped Grandad. "I can see why Captain Red wants to get his thieving hands on it now."

Vivid, heartfelt memories flooded back to me. The excitement of finding the map and then the treasure. The hurt and dismay when it was almost lost to the callous Captain Red and his pirates, and the elation and exhilaration when we escaped with it, and handed it back it to its rightful owners - Takootu and his people.

"No way Captain Red will ever get his hands on this again!" shouted Nino, swishing his Rodu through the air, like he was cutting Captain Red in half.

"Well said, young Nino," cried Grandad cheerfully.

"Your fearless guards will see to that."

After exploring a few more local sights we returned to eat at Hotel Zeo, where Grandma and Grandad were staying. As part of the special celebrations they were giving a spectacular feast of food – a bit like one of Grandma's famous afternoon teas but with no flapjack - SADLY!

Not all the dishes were amazing though – I gave the raw fish a miss, but the coconut milk and fresh fruit salad were heaven.

After the feast we were entertained by local musicians who played Polynesian instruments and then came the dancers. Dressed in exotic traditional costumes, dancers of all ages entertained us to vibrant rhythmical music. I got to play the drums for a short time and then Rai persuaded Minoo and Grandma to join in with the dancers and no one seemed to mind. It was extremely funny to watch.

"Minoo is a natural!" cried Rai, almost crying with laughter.

"Grandma's not bad either," chuckled Grandad, tapping his foot to the beat.

Thankfully Mum and Dad didn't join in the dancing as well. That would have been far too embarrassing. After a while, Takootu arrived and apologised for being away on our special welcome evening.

"You is having a nice time? Yes?"

We all assured him we were, and told him what we had been up to and how wonderful his people were.

"I am very pleased you is liking our home."

After more laughing and dancing, Nino asked Takootu if he and Rai could take us down to the beach to see his new canoe. Takootu didn't answer at first. He was busy talking to Dad about the design of the new museum.

"Please Papa," urged Rai, "Before it gets too dark! I want to show them Poe too. It's so hot in here."

"Yes OK, "replied Takootu, slightly wearily. "But just for half hour. Busy day tomorrow - for us all."

"Thanks Papa!" shouted, Rai and Nino giving Takootu

a big hug.

"Have fun and stay in lagoon!" added Takootu, firmly. "I is sending Mareva and Tametoa down in short while to check on you…"

"Bye Papa! Bye everyone!" shouted, Rai and Nino, making their way to the Hotel exit.

"Please don't go and steal my star dance partner – Minoo," smiled Grandma, blowing us all a kiss. "I'll be lost without him."

We all laughed and waved goodbye.

"You can carry on your dance tomorrow, Grandma," cried Jana, affectionately. "See you later!"

"Don't forget your Rodu - you two," reminded Nino, excitedly. "I've got some great new moves to show you…"

Chapter 16

Play Time

We ran down to the beach excitedly, practising a few battle moves on the way. The beach was close by and we were there in a matter of minutes.

"This is it," declared Nino, proudly pointing out his new canoe on the sand. "What do you think?"

It was about 3 metres long and was decorated with wonderful Polynesian patterns, similar to the tattoos we had seen on the Radi warriors.

"It's awesome!" I replied, feeling quite envious. "Can we try it out?"

"You bet!" replied Nino, excitedly. "Quick! Help me carry it down to the sea, before it gets too dark."

A few moments later we were all safely aboard, paddling around the turquoise blue lagoon. Nino had given us all an oar to paddle with – including Minoo, who didn't look totally sure what to do with it. In fact none of us were that sure. At the start we found steering VERY difficult and kept going round and round in circles, which made us all get a fit of the giggles!

"I said LEFT not RIGHT!" laughed Nino, bursting into hysterics.

We soon got the hang of it though, and started to do some really cool, fancy turns. The water was quite shallow and beautifully clear. We could see fish of all colours darting in and out of vision.

Then all of sudden, out from nowhere a blue dolphin soared high into the air, twirling magnificently. It was Poe! Seconds later Puati flew out of the water too! The dolphins jumped and chased each other around the canoe and under and over it too. It was so much fun to watch. Minoo was chattering excitedly, even more than usual.

It was a warm still evening, with just a hint of breeze. We could still hear music and happy voices coming from the shore. The sun was now a deep orange ball hovering above the horizon.

"This is the life…" I smiled, cheerfully humming a tune, with Minoo perched up high on my shoulders.

"Thank you for showing us your canoe," cried Jana, happily. "It's so perfect here..."

It really was the perfect evening. The sunset was like a painting Mum might have done.

"It's getting colder," said Rai, suddenly sounding slightly uneasy. "Papa would want us home now and besides I'm feeling something bad is about to happen…!"

"You and your sixth sense, Rai!" teased Nino. "Nothing bad is going to happen. It's a beautiful evening. Don't always go and spoil things!"

But all of a sudden the peaceful atmosphere was broken by a loud thumping of drums ringing out from the shore...

Chapter 17

Red's Revenge

"It's the ALARM!" shouted Nino, anxiously. "There must be a fire!"

"Or something worse..." gasped Rai. "Look! Over by the Museum..."

We all gazed back towards the Museum, which was high up on the cliff overlooking the harbour. All we could see was people running around in all directions, as though a bomb had just gone off.

"It must be the treasure!" cried Rai, nervously. "It's been stolen – I know it has..."

"That's impossible!" replied Nino, doubtfully. "There are more than thirty guards protecting it!"

At that moment we suddenly heard frantic shouts and voices close by. We looked around nervously to see

Tametoa and Mareva paddling their canoe like lightning across the water towards us. My heart raced. We were all in a panic. The next thing we knew, Mareva and Tametoa were beside us in their canoe, looking very agitated and upset.

"You must all go back to shore right NOW!" cried Mareva, with fear in her eyes.

"Why?" protested Nino. "What's happened..?"

"The TREASURE…!" replied Mareva desperately. "It's been stolen!"

We all froze and looked at each other opened mouthed…

Suddenly the low rattle of an outboard motor could be heard echoing across the bay.

"I bet that's them escaping!" cried Tametoa angrily.

I peered through my telescope anxiously …

It was getting quite gloomy now, but I could still make out the outline of a small boat racing across the bay at great speed. I adjusted the focus to get a closer look at the crew...

My heart sank instantly. It was a familiar face we knew only too well – a face you couldn't forget... menacing and wild ... It was Captain Red!

"It's HIM!" I cried dejectedly. "Captain Red and his cruel and cowardly crew. They've got the treasure!"

"NO!!!" cried, Tametoa, beside himself. "How can he have managed it...? IT'S IMPOSSIBLE..."

"Where are Papa and the warriors?" demanded Mareva, frantically. "Are they catching them...?"

I peered through my telescope again, uneasily.

"Yes," I replied, excitedly. "I can see them! There must be about twenty battle canoes giving chase. Takootu is out in front! But they are a long way behind."

"Papa will catch them!" cried Nino, confidently.

But the rest of us weren't so sure. Takootu and the Radi warriors were giving chase, but battle canoes although fast, were no match for a motor boat.

"They're heading for that ship!" cried Tametoa.

We all looked out to the east, and there on the horizon was a silhouette of a ship we had seen earlier that day. It was now very clear to see – it was Captain Red's galleon - the *Golden Age*.

"You were right!" gasped, Jana, her voice trembling with fear and terror.

"I wish I hadn't been" I replied, starting to feel desperate.

Soon Captain Red would have the treasure in the safety of his ship and it would be lost forever…

"I thought the Captain was supposed to believe in the

old pirate ways." cried Jana, furiously. "Not using speedy motor boats to escape – double-crossing cheater!

"Papa will never catch them now..." sighed Rai, dejectedly.

"Oh yes he might!" cried Mareva, suddenly sounding quite confident. "The treasure is heavy - it will take them time to winch it up off the boat. Papa might well catch them up. We can get there as well!

"It's closer to Red's ship from here too!" added Tametoa, enthusiastically.

"What are we waiting for then – let's go!" shouted Nino, excitedly.

"No Nino", cried Mareva, firmly. "You would not get there in time, and besides it is too dangerous for you. You must all return to shore. Tametoa and I will help Papa bring Zeo's Treasure back – do not fear…"

Nino didn't get time to argue his case. Mareva and Tametoa waved goodbye and raced off in their canoe at a blistering speed.

"That's not fair!" complained Nino. "We want to help out too. I'm fed up of being treated like a baby and missing out on all the adventure…"

"Me too!" frowned Rai.

I felt exactly the same as Nino and Rai, and I could tell from the look on Jana's face that she did too. We wanted to help get the treasure back more than anything. We knew the Captain and crew better than anyone else – we might be able to help Takootu…

But there was nothing we could do. We could never get there in time. We were too far away.

"I guess we'd better head back then…" said Jana, dejectedly.

"No wait!" cried Rai, excitedly. "I think I have an idea…"

Chapter 18

Poe Power

Rai made a sharp whistling noise and within a matter of seconds, Poe appeared once more, leaping across the water, closely followed by Puati.

"Poe! Poe!" cried Rai, excitedly. "I have a very important job for you."

As soon as Poe came alongside, Rai showed her the mooring rope which was attached to the front of Nino's canoe and pointed to her mouth. Poe squeaked twice as though she understood what Rai was asking her to do, and grasped the rope tightly with her snout.

Moments later we were racing over the open sea - Poe was PULLING us! It was like we were aboard our very own speed boat - it was breathtaking!

"Go POE!!" shouted Nino, as we sped towards the sinister dark shadow of Captain Red's galleon. "Hang on tight!"

"Fingers crossed, Mareva and Tametoa won't see us in the gloom," cried Rai, nervously.

We all nodded in agreement.

The sun was starting to set, but there was still just enough daylight to see what was going on. I peered through my telescope, my hand trembling with fright and excitement.

"I can see the treasure," I cried despondently. "They're starting to hoist it up on to the ship. We haven't got long!"

"Can you see Papa and the others?" shouted Nino. "Are they close?"

I peered through my telescope again…

"Yes - I see them! Takootu is still out in front. But they are still a long way off."

"NO!" sighed Nino, dejectedly. "The treasure will be on board by the time they get there!"

"Then we MUST do something to help!" I cried.

"What?" asked Jana desperately.

"I don't know. Get on board somehow and rescue the treasure…"

"How exactly…?" asked Jana.

"I haven't worked that bit out yet..." I replied, hopefully. "But there must be some way…"

"I have an idea…!" shouted Jana, excitedly. "We have a perfect diversion. The pirates will all be focused on the Radi closing in on them. So if we approach the *Golden Age* from the other side they won't even see us coming. We can climb aboard and rescue the treasure!"

"Brilliant plan, Jana!" I shouted, enthusiastically. "Let's

get to it…"

How we were actually going to get on board and rescue the treasure was another question, but we didn't have time to worry about that yet…

Suddenly there was a deafening explosion from the deck of the *Golden Age* and a huge black ball blasted its way towards the oncoming Radi.

"Cannon fire!" screamed Rai, fearfully.

Chapter 19

Jittery Jana

"It's going to make it impossible for them to get close to the ship now." sighed Nino, desperately, as the cannon ball hit the water well short of the Radi battle canoes. "They're going to be blown out of the water!"

Nino was right. The task for Takootu and his Radi warriors had just become ten times more difficult - not to mention a hundred times more dangerous. But at least they were out of range for the moment.

"WE'RE going to be blasted out of the water too, if we don't get a move on." cried Jana, urgently. "Come on!"

Poe steered our canoe speedily around the back of the *Golden Age* until we were in touching distance. The elation of reaching the vessel was short lived, as we surveyed our next challenge. The sides of the ship were almost vertical and as tall as a house!

"How are we going to get up THERE?" asked Jana, going into a panic.

Before we had time to think, Minoo sprang off my shoulder (where he had been hanging on for dear life for the last few minutes) and scampered up onto the deck, like he was shinning up a palm tree on Island Zeo.

"Clever Minoo," whispered, Rai.

Suddenly I noticed a coil of rope hanging over the side rail and motioned to Minoo. He squeaked excitedly and threw the rope down to us, looking ever so pleased with himself.

"Very clever, Minoo!" encouraged Rai.

I pulled on the rope and tested it would take our weight. It held fast.

Now it was our turn to get up on deck.

"You expect ME to climb up there?!" inquired Jana, looking absolutely petrified. "Are you CRAZY?!"

Jana hated the idea of climbing up a tree in the back garden, but this was in another league. It was like going up the north face of Everest with a swirling wind and a choppy ocean below us – it was SCARY! But Jana knew she would have to be braver than usual, if we had any chance of rescuing back the treasure.

"I'm right behind you!" I whispered reassuringly, as Jana started her ascent.

"You'd better be!" replied Jana, her voice quivering with fear, as she climbed ever so cautiously up the rope.

Nino was leading with Rai close behind. He loved climbing as much as me and Minoo, but this climb was going to be different. One false move would lead to DISASTER and we would all be plummeting down into the ocean…

The wind howled and the *Golden Age* pitched from side-to-side and up and down in the ever increasing swell.

"Hang on tight, Jana!" I cried urgently.

"I AM, Jay!!" she replied, sounding terrified.

Jana had good reason to be feeling frightened. It was one of the most dangerous things we'd ever done, but we had no choice. We had to get up on deck to have a chance of rescuing the treasure… Thankfully, we didn't have far to go now. I could see Minoo at the top, chattering cheerfully and encouraging us all on.

"Almost there! Keep going everyone!"

Within a matter of minutes (which actually seemed more like hours) we were all safely up on deck hiding in the shadows.

SOMEHOW we had made it.

Jana had shocked me with her bravery. We all hugged each other in celebration and relief, but there was no time to lose. Rai looked back down to Poe, who was still swimming close to Nino's canoe, which we had tied-up to the *Golden Age*.

"We couldn't have done it without you," she whispered, blowing her a big kiss. "Stay close with

Puati – we will be back soon with the treasure - hopefully…"

"Yes let's get on with it!" whispered Nino, excitedly. "I'm sure the treasure will be aboard by now."

But just as we were about to start exploring, we heard the sound of loud, rough voices approaching rapidly. We needed to hide somewhere quickly – but where…? Just one clumsy sound and we would all be discovered...

Chapter 20

Under Fire

We held our breath and prayed we wouldn't be seen, as we huddled together in the corner of an old rowing boat. Eventually the sound of voices grew softer and softer, so we peeped over the top to see if the coast was clear...

Thankfully... it was!

Although we were still nervous of being seen, we started searching all over the deck for the treasure. We kept to the shadows, but sadly there was no sign of it anywhere.

"They must have stored it down below," sighed Nino.

Suddenly I heard a voice that made my whole body shudder. It was CAPTAIN RED...

There he stood at the helm, sinister and threatening with a large black patch covering his left eye. He was a giant of a man, with wild looking hair and a formidable dark beard that made him look even more menacing.

"Don't waste your cannons - you dim-witted dummies! They are STILL out of range."

"Aye aye, Captain," came the sheepish reply from the crew.

"Wait for my order…" snarled the Captain, laughing insanely, and thrusting his giant sword to the heavens. "Soon they be close enough and we will BLOW them out of the ocean!!"

Things looked bad - VERY bad. In a matter of minutes poor Takootu and the Radi warriors would be in range of the cannons and the consequences were too grim to think about. There was no time to lose - we had to do something to save them... but what? There were too many pirates to overpower them, even though Nino couldn't wait to show off his fierce fighting skills.

The wind howled and the ship started to groan as it swayed backwards and forwards in the heavy swell. It felt like a BIG storm was brewing...

"The cannon ball store!" whispered Nino suddenly, pointing to massive stack of cannon balls at the stern of the ship.

"What about it?" asked Jana blankly.

"It's where the pirates store them. All we have to do is drop them ALL over the side and they'll have no ammunition!" explained Nino, excitedly.

He was right. It was the store. We watched nervously as a huge hairy pirate picked a cannon ball up and carried it back down to one of the cannons. They looked

REALLY heavy!

We all glanced at Nino again, doubtfully. It was a great plan, apart from the fact that the cannon balls would weigh a TON! We might struggle to pick up even ONE let alone a hundred of them! What's more, even if we could, they would make a massive noise when we threw them overboard.

"Well has anyone else got a better idea?" replied Nino, defensively.

We didn't. It was the only plan we had. We just needed more muscle. We'd all had fun lifting heavy bowling balls at friends' birthday parties, but this was going to be VERY different. The odds of pulling it off were looking extremely unlikely. Then just at that moment we suddenly heard a rustling noise coming from behind us. We all turned around anxiously, fearing the worst, with our Rodu held high ready for battle…

Chapter 21

Now or Never

But to our utter surprise and relief it wasn't Captain
Red or any of his cruel, callous pirates - it was Mareva
and Tametoa!

"Oops!" cried Nino, realising who it was too late to pull
out of his strike.

"What are YOU doing here?" gasped Mareva, looking
surprised, angry and concerned all at the same time, as
she ducked to avoid Nino's frenzied Rodu attack.
"You're supposed to be home in Radimatu?!"

"Mareva!" gasped Rai, embracing her warmly. "Thank
goodness you are here – we need your help - now! Papa
is in great danger..."

We apologised and explained what we had done and
what we needed to do NOW if Takootu and his brave
warriors were to be saved...

"It's a brilliant plan, Nino," whispered Mareva, calmly. "Zeo and Papa would be proud of your ingenuity and bravery but disobeying your older sister was wrong – don't do it again please – or you Rai. We help you now – then we find the treasure!"

Nino gave me a smirk of pride. I think he thought he was in for more of a ticking off. With Tametoa and Mareva to help us our plan certainly looked more possible.

"Two more minutes and the Radi scum will be in range!" laughed Captain Red, menacingly. "The treasure is ours and soon there will be no one to come after us!"

Rai looked close to tears. It was now or never! Without delay we all sneaked over towards the cannon ball store and ducked down low. The storm was raging now. The wind was fierce and we could hear thunder rumbling close by.

"Wait for the next lightning bolt," whispered Tametoa. "The thunder clap will come a few seconds after – then we throw them overboard."

"Any minute now," cried Captain Red, gleefully. "Prime the cannons!"

We didn't have to wait long for lightning to illuminate the sky. We paused as instructed, and then Tametoa gave the signal to move as the thunder started to clatter...

The cannon balls DID weigh a ton! It felt like our arm muscles were going to burst, but we had to keep going. Thankfully, Tametoa and Mareva were working at great speed. They seemed to be picking up the cannon balls like they were small coconuts and tossing them over the side!

Unfortunately, by the time the thunder had subsided there were still dozens of cannon balls left in the store.

"Prepare to FIRE!" ordered Captain Red, forcefully.

"We need to keep going," whispered Mareva, urgently. "They won't notice them dropping overboard in this gale."

So that's what we did. In the next few moments, cannon ball after cannon ball was dumped over the side of the *Golden Age* until there was just one left, which Tametoa hurled overboard triumphantly.

I couldn't believe it - we had done it!

"Well done, everyone!" whispered Mareva, as we all crept back to our safe spot near the stern of the ship.

Although we had done well, the pirates still had a dirty great big cannon ball primed and ready to fire in EVERY one of their cannons. They also had a second, resting at the side of the cannon, all set for loading. Only after they had fired them both would the cannons be out of ammunition…

"Let's pray they miss Papa and the Radi with their first two volleys…" whispered Mareva nervously, her eyes fixed on the fast-approaching battle canoes…

Chapter 22

Sitting Ducks

Can you see them?" whispered, Tametoa anxiously.

I gazed nervously through my telescope in the dim light. Takootu and the Radi warriors were now only fifty or so metres away. They were such easy targets now, the pirates couldn't miss.

They really were sitting ducks...

"FIRE FIRE FIRE!" screamed the Captain sternly, looking crazier than ever.

We all held our breath anxiously and prayed that the first two barrages would be unsuccessful. I squinted through my telescope, nervously. The sun had set a few minutes earlier, but there was still just enough light to see what was happening...

Bright flashes of fire lit up the deck like a firework

display on Bonfire night, as a double volley of cannon balls were sent hurtling towards the defenceless Radi canoes. The sea exploded like a bubbling stream of larva, as the cannon balls crashed into the surface and we began to fear the worst.

Three battle canoes capsised instantly as the sea reared up like a mini tidal wave. But to our relief and astonishment there were no direct hits! Takootu and most of the Radi canoes were mercifully still afloat and now only a matter of metres away.

"DUMHEADED DIMWITS!" cursed Captain Red. "You missed them again."

Takootu's battle canoe was still leading the way – they would be with us incredibly soon…

"Reload immediately!" raged the Captain, looking incensed. "And don't you dare miss them this time or you will ALL be walking the plank!"

"Aye aye, "Captain Red, replied the crew fearfully.

We all watched nervously as several of the pirates raced

down to the store to get more ammunition. When they saw that the store was empty their faces were a picture…

"Get on with it you half-witted boneheads!" roared Captain Red. "They will be on us in a matter of seconds!"

"Sorry, Captain," replied a giant looking pirate, with a ring through his nose. "The store is empty – the cannon balls are all gone…"

"ALL GONE!!" roared the Captain, going into frenzy. "Impossible! You dim-witted donkey – there must be at least two hundred…"

Suddenly Captain Red stopped in mid sentence as he stared into the empty cannon ball store with a bemused and bewildered expression over his face.

"I smell a RAT!!" bellowed the Captain, looking around the deck suspiciously. "I'll wager we have a few stowaways on board… "Come out you yellow-bellied scoundrels and show yourselves!"

That was it. We were discovered. What would become of us now…? We huddled together in the shadows awaiting our fate. Would they slit our throats or make us walk the plank...?

Either way, things didn't look good for us. But at least our plan had worked and for the moment at least, the Radi and Takootu still had a chance.

Chapter 23

Battle Stations

Thankfully for us, Captain Red had something else to bother with, as Takootu and the Radi were now just below us.

"They're scaling the starboard side, Captain!" screamed a young pirate voice high up in the crow's nest.

"Devil and Doubloons!" cursed the Captain, crashing his sword into the main mast in anger. "We will deal with the stowaways later… BATTLE STATIONS!"

"Papa will save us now!" cried Nino, excitedly.

Suddenly there seemed to be pirates swarming everywhere. I recognised a few from our adventure last year, including the first mate and the cabin girl. Within a few seconds they had formed a long line along the starboard side of the ship. There they waited menacingly – peering over the side - weapons at the ready...

Tametoa was restless and wanted to join in the fight, but Mareva pulled him back.

"Not yet, brave Tametoa. Be patient. We stay here for now..."

Tametoa didn't question Mareva's decision and we all stayed silent and still, as we watched from the shadows. I was starting to feel incredibly anxious for Takootu and his Radi warriors. We knew how steep the side of the ship was. The pirates were above them and armed. How were they all going to get up onto deck?

"The Booty is ours and ours it will stay!" bellowed the Captain, twirling his cutlass above his head, boldly. "Fight for each other and die for each other!"

The pirates cheered and jeered defiantly - they looked hungry for battle. The next few minutes went by in a frenzy. Lightning fired the sky and thunder claps rattled above us. There were shouts and cries and Captain Red barked out order upon order to his crew. The Radi warriors threw up grappling hooks to secure their ropes, and soon dozens of them were bravely climbing up the sheer side of the galleon.

"They be coming!" yelled Captain Red fiercely. "Be you ready!!"

As soon as the Radi reached the summit they were set upon by Captain Red and his bloodthirsty pirates. Warrior after warrior was sent plunging back down into the choppy, dark ocean below – much to the delight of the pirates.

"I thought the Radi were supposed to be fierce fighters?!" gloated the Captain, as he smacked another warrior with his sword into the depths beneath. "

"Papa will still save us!" whispered Rai, apprehensively.

But I wasn't feeling so sure.

The Radi were being picked off with ease – it was painful to watch. There was no sign of Takootu and none of his warriors had even set foot on deck!

"We must do something!" cried Tametoa, getting to his

feet. "We can't just sit here and watch them destroy us..."

"Yes. Now is the time," replied Mareva, with fire in her eyes. "If we can distract the pirates, even for a few seconds, it might make the difference! We must try..."

"We're coming too!" cried Nino, his Rodu primed for battle.

"And me," cried, Rai.

"And us!" I shouted, grasping my Rodu tightly.

"No," said Mareva firmly. "You must ALL stay here hiding. It is too dangerous. Papa would want it this way. He thinks you are home safe. Tametoa and I have trained for this moment – it is our duty to try and help."

Nino said nothing. None of us did. I could tell by the look on his face that he knew Mareva was right. She hugged him and Rai tightly and then flew into battle with Tametoa close behind her...

Chapter 24

Sprat Attack

"ARGH!" came the agonising cry, as another Radi warrior was swiped mercilessly from the ship.

"This be too easy," chuckled Captain Red with delight. "There will be nothing left of them at this rate!"

At that moment, Mareva and Tametoa appeared on deck and went straight into battle, with their Rodu twirling around their heads like lightsabers. The pirates were caught off guard and were hit by several solid blows.

"Bosh and Hogwash!" yelled the Captain angrily. "Young stowaways on deck - capture them now!"

But Mareva and Tametoa had other ideas, and

continued to battle on bravely, taking on pirate after pirate, and using all their super-fast, ninja-like skills that Takootu had taught them.

"He's mine!" shouted, Mareva, as she dispatched another big hairy pirate into the ocean.

Suddenly, I noticed Minoo out on deck too. He was swinging up high on the rigging and then flying down on top of the pirates' heads! It was annoying them intensely and making it difficult for them to see – he was being so brave.

"Surround them you yellow-bellied dimwits!" raged Captain Red. "These young sprats be making monkeys out of you."

The pirates did what their Captain had ordered, but as they did gaps started to appear in their defence on the starboard side and within seconds the first Radi warrior emerged on deck!

"Devil and Doubloons!" cursed Captain Red angrily. "Back to your stations you dim-witted dodo's. They're getting through... STOP them!"

"Aye aye, Captain."

"Papa will save us, NOW…" smiled Rai, excitedly.

The plan was working! If only, Mareva, Tametoa and Minoo could keep going for a few seconds longer…

But just at that moment things took a dramatic turn for the worse. All of a sudden, one of the pirates hurled a huge fishing net over Mareva and Tametoa and THAT was IT! They were caught – trapped like flapping fish from the ocean, powerless to move.

"Good work, Black." laughed a jubilant Captain. "Tie them to the mast!"

Poor Mareva and Tametoa, they had fought so bravely. We suddenly felt lost again. There was still no sign of Takootu and now brave Mareva and Tametoa were captured. As for Minoo – he could be stranded somewhere on deck injured or worse. All their efforts had been in vain. Or had they…?

"Look!" cried Jana, pointing ecstatically towards the starboard side, where a few more Radi had managed to sneak aboard. "It's Takootu!"

"Papa!" gasped Rai, excitedly. "I knew he would save us."

Our spirits lifted instantly – now Takootu was on board anything was possible.

"SCURVY DOGS!" raged Captain Red, furiously, moving towards Takootu. "Slay him - now!"

But Chief Takootu had other ideas. Soon it was the pirates who were being whacked overboard by Takootu and his brave Radi warriors. The pirates looked clumsy and slow compared to the warriors lightning-quick skills.

"I said FINISH him! You cowardly yellow-bellies!" screeched the Captain, as Takootu skillfully dodged a knife attack and sent another pirate overboard screaming for his mamma.

"I told you Papa would come," smiled Rai, her face full of joy.

"Now he will show them who is boss!" cried Nino,

excitedly.

The tide was definitely turning...

Could we dare to start believing that Takootu and his brave warriors could actually do it? Save us all and win back Zeo's Treasure…??

Chapter 25

Blackmail

"ENOUGH!!" bellowed Captain Red, waving his sword menacingly from his new vantage point, high up on the rigging.

"Surrender now Takootu or we will have to DEAL immediately with your two brave, young warriors..."

We squinted through the gloom and there by the main mast we could just make out Mareva and Tametoa. They were both being held at knife point by a hideously mean looking pirate dressed all in black!

Takootu must have seen them too. He stopped fighting instantly, and so did the two Radi warriors who had managed to get aboard. Takootu then moved purposefully towards the two young warriors who he recognised and knew so well. We could see the panic and concern in his eyes.

"Wise choice, my old friend," taunted the Captain, as he pointed his sword menacingly towards Mareva and Tametoa.

"It would be a shame to lose such courageous, young fighters like these over a misunderstanding about the treasure."

Takootu did not reply. He looked awkwardly towards Mareva and back towards the Captain. He looked trapped...

"Now you will retreat, Chief Takootu, and give up this pathetic attack. Then the young sprats will live to tell the story of this famous night - the night the Bandi won back what is rightfully ours – Blackbeard's Treasure! "

The pirates cheered and laughed excitedly, waving their weapons in the air triumphantly.

"It Zeo's Treasure – not Blackbeard's!" cried Nino, angrily, jumping up to do battle.

"No!" said Rai, pulling him back. "There are too many of them. Papa has enough to deal with now they have Mareva and Tametoa."

"Rai is right," whispered Jana, persuasively. "We will only get caught. If we stay hidden we might be able to help the others escape and find the treasure."

Nino sat back down reluctantly.

While all this had been going on, I suddenly noticed Minoo perched right at the top of the main mast. Thank goodness he was safe. He was looking extremely mischievous, as though he was about to do something dangerous. Maybe he was looking for the treasure or trying to help Takootu? I hoped he would be alright…

Meanwhile, Captain Red was waiting impatiently for Takootu to answer his question.

"Well, old man, what's it going to be? Retreat now or have young blood on your hands… I haven't got all night?!"

The pirates jeered again jubilantly.

Takootu stood motionless. I could tell from the look on his face that he wanted to smash the Captain flying into the Pacific Ocean, but he just couldn't risk Mareva and Tametoa being hurt. He listened to the pirates jeering and laughing at him and eventually he spoke...

"OK Captain, you win. I agree your deal." Takootu paused, his voice trembling with emotion. "We is retreating and we be leaving you with Zeo's Treasure, but only IF you is releasing the young Radi - right NOW!"

"No, I don't think so." replied the Captain, starting to chuckle in his typical sinister manner. "We be holding all the ACES! If we give you the young sprats now, you be chasing us around all the islands in the South Pacific 'til you be getting the treasure back. I ain't dumb you know."

The pirates jeered and laughed again.

Takootu didn't reply. I'm sure he could think of lots of adjectives to describe Captain Red, but dumb was not one of them.

Thunder clattered overhead and lightning lit up the sky once more. The tension was unbearable. What could Takootu do now...? What was to become of us all...?

Suddenly the Captain climbed back down from the rigging and moved right up close to Takootu.

"I'm sure we can come to some amicable arrangement, Chief Takootu. We don't want no more blood spilled tonight, if we can avoid it - do we now...?"

The Captain paused and then came even closer to Takootu.

"I be willing to release these two young sprats, after you have retreated, but not until we do sail somewhere SAFE – then I do release them..."

"No," replied Takootu, desperately. "I give you word. Word of Takootu... Chief of Radimatu – leader of the Radi - I is not coming after the treasure... release the young Radi now and we go..."

"Stone the crow's nest!" replied the Captain, incredulously. "You and your fearless warriors are prepared to give up the treasure – treasure you and your kinfolk have spent centuries searching for – for these two young sprats…?"

"Yes. You is having my word… Release the young Radi and we go." repeated Takootu desperately." You keep treasure!"

"No Papa!" came a frantic scream from Tametoa. "Don't give up the treasure for us!"

A look of horror suddenly shot across Takootu's face. His secret of all secrets was OUT…!

A gasp of astonishment rippled around the crew.

The Captain didn't waste much time in pressing home his advantage…

"PAPA…!" taunted the Captain excitedly, looking like he had just won the Pirate lottery. "Looks like we have struck luckier than I thought, men. No wonder the Chief wants them back so - they be his own flesh and blood! I thought the boy looked annoyingly familiar and the girl fights like she is his blood too. Now we have double the booty, men. Now we be carrying extra plunder in the hold. Our cargo has just quadrupled in value!!"

The pirates cheered and jeered even louder than before.

Things looked bad, in fact, they had never looked worse for us. Now it was going to be almost impossible for Takootu to bargain with the Captain.

Takootu looked beaten - powerless to do anything ...

Chapter 26

Deadly Duel

But just at that moment I spotted Minoo chattering at the top of the mast, looking extremely excited about something. I peered through my telescope to get a closer view and suddenly I noticed something AMAZING...!

Mareva and Tametoa were no longer tied to the mast. Somehow they had managed to get free and something was telling me that Minoo had A LOT to do with it!

They both looked determined and ready for battle. Tametoa's first swipe took out the hideously mean pirate guarding them, whose attention seemed momentarily distracted by the crew's recent excitement at the expense of poor Takootu.

"We're FREE, Papa!" cried Mareva, knocking another pirate to the ground with a skilful twirl of her Rodu. "Get the Captain!"

"SCURVY DOGS!" screeched Captain Red, going into a panic. "How did they escape? Capture them!"

But Takootu had other ideas and in a flash he was over by their sides defending them.

"Stay close to me!" he ordered, giving them both a warm fatherly embrace. "We protect you now. We is fighting them together!"

The two Radi warriors had joined them, and instantly formed a protective ring around Mareva and Tametoa – not that they really needed protecting the way they were fighting.

"GET THEM!" raged Captain Red.

The odds still didn't look good - five Radi against more than thirty pirates, but it WAS Takootu. We had to believe it was possible...

It was almost dark now. A crescent moon shone

weakly, glinting through the cracks in the dark storm clouds. The wind howled menacingly and the rain hammered down onto the deck.

"Slay them all!" yelled the Captain, waving his sword wildly in the moonlight. "The booty is ours, men. Fight bravely, like the pirates from the Golden Age. Fight for each other and die for each other!"

The crew cheered loudly and flew into battle again. Soon the pirates were coming at Takootu from all directions. Giant ones, ugly ones, wild ones, bearded ones – not to mention really fierce ones – they were totally outnumbered!

They attacked with knives and long swords, but each time they struck they were successfully repelled by

Takootu and his skillful Radi warriors.

"Great work!" cried Takootu, expertly dispatching another hapless pirate into the ocean. "Stay close, everyone."

But Captain Red wasn't so impressed with his crew.

"BOSH and HOGWASH!" he raged. "Stop quivering like jelly fish you big yellow-bellies! Fight like MEN. There be only five of them!"

More and more pirates joined the attack, but the result was just the same. Takootu and his mini fighting team kept going - swatting off the pirates like they were flies round a dinner plate.

"Nice shot!" cried Mareva, as Tametoa smashed another pirate flying over the side.

Captain Red was looking increasingly exasperated by his crew's feeble efforts and decided to take matters into his own hands. All of a sudden, he leapt down from high up on the rigging and before we knew it, he and Takootu were locked into a deadly duel...!

"Time to die, Chief Takootu..!" cried the Captain, looking scarier than I had ever seen him before. "You had your chance to retreat - now you will pay…"

The Captain looked fierce and formidable, as he swished his huge razor-sharp sword through the cool night air. Thunder rumbled in the distance and flashes of lightning lit up the old galleon making it look like something out of a horror movie!

Takootu was a master technician with his weapon and he needed to be, as he parried vicious attack after vicious attack from the powerful Captain. They fought continuously around the deck … up high, down low… ducking and diving to avoid each other's blows…

Captain Red knew that if he could defeat Takootu, the treasure would be his. Likewise, Takootu knew that if he could somehow defeat Captain Red his family would be saved and so would the treasure. We were all praying that Takootu would come through for us. If he didn't, everything was lost…

The pirates looked on and jeered as Takootu stumbled

and looked like he was tiring.

"Had enough, old man..?" jibed the Captain, thundering his sword down inches from Takootu's head.

"Never!" replied Takootu defiantly, as he successfully deflected another thrust to his heart.

"Be careful, Papa!" cried Mareva.

Takootu was far from finished. Suddenly he seemed to get a second wind. He was now on the offensive, twirling his Rodu expertly through the air and striking the Captain with lightning quick blows to his arms and body.

"Get him Papa!" cried Nino, excitedly.

Now it was the Captain who was backing off and defending for his life. He was edging closer and closer to the side of the ship...

Suddenly, the Captain let out a loud cry of anguish, as he was caught on the hand by a thunderous strike from Takootu. The Captain's cutlass crashed to the ground and with it the pirate's hopes seemed dashed. The

Captain looked back up at Takootu, in surprise and bewilderment, as though he couldn't believe that he had lost.

But just at that moment, something truly dreadful happened…

There was an earsplitting bang and a dazzling flash of light, which seemed to be coming from the direction of one of the pirates. The mean sinister pirate dressed all in black, who was standing very close to the Captain. Takootu let out an agonising cry and slumped backwards on to the side rail – just inches from the sheer edge of the galleon.

It looked like he'd been SHOT!

"Papa!" cried Nino and Rai, looking totally distraught.

The crew gasped in shock and excitement…

"Perfect timing, Black" sneered the Captain, retrieving his sword from the deck, and moving purposefully over to the injured and now defenceless Takootu. Before Takootu had time to react, the callous Captain gave him an almighty shove, which sent him plummeting over the edge and into the dark depths below…

"Goodnight Takootu …" waved the Captain, smirking gleefully. "Revenge is so sweet...!"

The crew gasped once more. Then a tremendous cheer of excitement and celebration rippled around the *Golden Age* filling the night air.

There was nothing we could do. We all watched on - devastated … stunned...

Prickly-Pong Island

&

The Revenge of Captain Red

PART 2

Chapter 1

No Hope

We were still in a state of shock as we huddled together below deck, imprisoned in the ship's stronghold. It was dark and damp. The only light came from a lantern in the distance.

It hadn't taken long for the pirates to find us once Takootu had been defeated. We had all put up a bit of a fight with Nino leading the way. We had managed to land a few hostile blows with our Rodu, but it was to no avail - there were too many of them.

Tametoa and Mareva had been captured too, but the Radi warriors had managed to dive overboard after poor Takootu. We all hoped and prayed that they had been successful in rescuing him. To think otherwise was just too unthinkable.

Two hefty pirates guarded our escape – not that escape from the ship was even possible. The storm was raging, even stronger than before. The wind was howling, the rain was lashing down and the *Golden Age* was pitching up and down on the giant waves, like a runaway rollercoaster ride.

I still couldn't believe what had happened earlier. I felt dazed, almost numb and looking at the others they did too. Everyone was silent, even Nino - not a word.

We were all feeling desperate and scared. We were captives on board a pirate ship with no hope in the world. The treasure had been stolen. The Radi had been beaten and Takootu...? Poor, brave Tookutu had been shot and dumped into the ocean like a piece of old, unwanted furniture. Would we ever see him again...?

Minoo sensed our mood. He snuggled up close to me and Jana. I could feel his little heart beating softly. He seemed to know we were all in a state of trauma.

"Do not despair," whispered Mareva, quietly. "Papa is strong. Our warriors will rescue him and he will recover quickly. Tomorrow he will out be out in the battle canoes searching for us and find us he will!"

I was staggered and cheered by Mareva's confidence and positivity. Takootu certainly was a very special person; if anyone could come back from such a predicament it would be him.

We just hoped and prayed that Mareva was right.

Chapter 2

Storm Zeo

"Change course!" came the bellowing voice of Captain Red from above. "The storm is too strong. Head north for the first island we see."

"What about the Radi, Captain?" inquired a husky pirate voice.

"The Radi?" laughed Captain Red. "They not be following us in this tempest and besides, the Radi be ALL gone! DEAD at the bottom of the ocean and so be their precious leader."

The Captain let out a triumphant laugh and all the pirates started to jeer and cheer with him. This was too much for Tametoa. He looked like he was going to explode and pulled at the chain that was binding us, like a caged tiger.

"Stay calm, Tametoa." whispered Mareva, kindly, giving him a gentle hug. "Do not believe the Captain's words. He is wrong. Papa and the Radi are not finished and never will be - and he knows it."

Tametoa stopped struggling and Mareva continued.

"This is good news. Zeo has sent the storm to help us – he is ANGRY. The storm is so powerful now that we are heading for the first island we come to, so we will still be close to Radimatu."

"You're right, Mareva!" replied Tametoa, suddenly sounding more optimistic. "Zeo is with us. We will be closer for when they come looking tomorrow. The treasure is not lost and neither is Papa. He is a warrior and will come through for us. We must be ready and stay strong like he would expect."

"Yes Papa will come for us - that I am sure," whispered Rai, with tears still in her eyes. "I feel it…"

"Yes Papa will come and will smash Captain Red into

the ocean!" cried Nino, passionately.

"Quiet!" whispered Mareva, looking alarmed. "If they know that the Chief of the Radi is your Papa too we will be in even more danger.

Mareva was right. We didn't want to give the merciless Captain any more advantage than he had already.

Chapter 3

Mutiny

A short while later we started to hear loud, gruff voices approaching from up on deck. It was a group of pirates coming down below and it looked and sounded like they were carrying something heavy. A tall thin pirate led the way, I recognised him from our last trip - it was the Captain's first mate. He had a long thin moustache and a patch over his right eye. The cabin girl was there too, carrying a lantern.

All of a sudden we realised what it was that they were carrying ... the TREASURE! Zeo's Treasure! It must have been hidden up on deck all this time.

We huddled together and pretended to be fast asleep, but I managed to keep half an eye open to see what was going on, and I'm sure the others were doing just the same. The pirates sighed with exhaustion as they laid the treasure chest down and started to look inside.

"Look!" cried the biggest and ugliest looking one, with a ring through his nose. "There must be hundreds of gold Doubloons in here! Not to mention the rubies, diamonds and pearls!"

"Take your thieving hands off it, Benito!" barked the first mate, irritably.

"All right, Marcus. Keep your hair on," replied Benito, closing the lid. "I only be looking."

"Over there," replied the first mate curtly, pointing to where he wanted the chest moved to. "And make it snappy!"

The pirates did as they were instructed.

"It's not fair, Marcus," moaned Benito, wiping the sweat from his brow. "Why do we have to share the treasure with the Bandi? We be the ones who did risk our precious necks stealing it off the Radi - NOT they! Crawling through them tiny underground tunnels – we could have got stuck down there forever. I say we deserve it all."

The other pirates murmured in agreement and started to pass around a large bottle of rum, which one of our guards had handed them.

So that's how the pirates managed to get in and steal the treasure – through the underground TUNNELS!

"Is this you or the rum talking?" inquired Marcus, sternly. "Don't let the Captain hear you muttering such nonsense – you remember what he done to you last time?"

Benito laughed and took another large swig out of the bottle.

I could remember what the Captain had done to him all right. It was one of the scariest things I'd ever seen in my entire life. He almost cut both his ears clean off! I wondered whether the pirate had learnt his lesson.

"Who are these Bandi people, anyways?" Benito continued, taking another large gulp from the bottle. "And what be so special about they?"

"The Bandi, as you know well enough Benito, are the oldest band of pirates that ever sailed these seas - more than 300 years ago. They be the ones who were led by HIM - the meanest of all us pirates that ever lived!"

"Blackbeard...?" inquired a fat-faced pirate with an earring through his nose.

"Yes Blackbeard, sailor," continued the first mate, "commonly known as Edward Teach – a bit of a wild lad from our home town, Bristol by all accounts."

"Give over, Marcus - you're having a laugh!" chuckled Benito. "You don't believe that rubbish do you? Next thing you'll be telling us that the Captain be Blackbeard's long lost cousin…"

The other pirates started to laugh out loud, but then, all of a sudden, they stopped abruptly and their expression turned to one of terror and panic...

"MUTINY and musketeers!" bellowed Captain Red, suddenly appearing from out of the shadows like a frenzied werewolf.

Benito looked scared out of his wits and dropped the bottle of rum to the floor, where it smashed into pieces...

"You dare to question the truth about the Bandi and MY ancestors' bloodline?" raged the Captain, swishing his cutlass wildly towards Benito's face. "That I, Redmond, Oliver Teach is a direct descendent to the meanest, most notorious pirate that ever lived!?"

"Sorry, Captain," stammered Benito, trembling with fear. "I…I..I.. was just having a laugh with the lads. Of course I believe it - you even do look like him."

The Captain looked mildly pleased at this last remark, but his mood swiftly passed.

"Bootlicking won't get you out of this defiance - you sniffling TRAITOR!" The Captain thrust his cutlass towards the terrified pirate's heart. "You will be sorry, sailor - very sorry. It be clear you can't hold your rum or your tongue – you're nothing more than a mutinous conspirator! Hold him still, first mate."

The first mate did as he was ordered.

"A sailor who can't hold his rum or his tongue is a menace to us all. Perhaps I will just have to cut your traitorous tongue out altogether - open wide…"

"NO..NO… NO!!!" pleaded Benito, desperately. "Please Captain, be merciful. I'm sorry - give me another chance…"

The other pirates could hardly bear to watch and neither could we. Benito continued to plead for his life as the Captain's sword moved closer and closer to its intended target...

Suddenly the razor sharp edge of his blade sliced into the top lip of the traumatised pirate and blood started to gush over his chin and onto the deck below…

Thankfully for Benito, the Captain showed mercy and suddenly stopped his attack, pulling his sword away moodily. "Oh stop blubbering like a baby you sniffling deserter – it be only a nick! Next time I WILL cut it out! As for now, I think it fitting we use one of the punishments from the Golden Age of pirates…"

"Aye aye Captain" replied the first mate.

"I warned you before Benito, not long since – now you will pay. String him up by his feet from the main mast, men. The old ways be the best!"

"Aye aye Captain!" cried the crew, excitedly.

A look of terror shot over Benito's face as the men grabbed him and frog-marched him up on deck. It wasn't long before his screams could be heard above the waves and howling wind.

"Let that be a lesson to all of you," warned the Captain. "And that includes you – young sprats!" He turned menacingly towards us and looked into our eyes. "Don't you be getting any ideas of doing anything stupid or you will end up the same as he... got it?"

We all nodded nervously. There was no way any of us wanted to be strung up like Benito. But Mareva didn't appear to be feeling as anxious as the rest of us.

"We won't insult you and your family Captain Red," replied Mareva, bravely. "But in return, I hope you will respect our family and the promise you gave to my father."

"My promise..?" replied the Captain curtly, looking surprised by Mareva's directness.

"Yes Captain, you told my father that you will release us as soon as you get to a safe place, remember?"

"Did I now..?" retorted the Captain, defensively. "Maybe I did... But we not be at a safe place yet, and I doubt we ever will be for a long, long time coming - months and months – years and years... probably NEVER!!"

The pirates jeered and laughed mockingly.

Mareva looked upset and angry, but didn't reply.

This only confirmed what we already knew – that Captain Red was not a man of his word and could NEVER be trusted. The only way we were going to get off this wretched ship was if somehow we were rescued or miraculously managed to escape.

Chapter 4

Wrecking Rocks

A few minutes later there was a huge jolt and a loud crashing sound…

"We've HIT something, Captain!" came the fearful cry from up on deck. "Must be rocks or a hidden reef – we didn't see it in this squall."

"Devil and Doubloons!" cursed Captain Red, rushing back up on deck. "What be the damage?"

"The underbelly, Captain!" screamed a nervous reply, through the howling wind and rain. "On the port side - we're taking in water."

"Scurvy dogs!" bellowed the Captain angrily. "All hands on deck. Get us to shore, bosun – before we sink!"

We couldn't see much from down below, but we could

feel the panic amongst the crew as they raced up on deck to assist.

"This is good news for us," whispered Tametoa. "Now we will be even closer to Radimatu."

"Not if we SINK!" cried Jana, looking terrified.

Jana was right to be alarmed. Suddenly we all had good reason to be afraid of something even more frightening than Captain Red. If the ship went down, we were done for...

"Look for the deep water, bosun." cried the Captain, urgently. "She won't stand another hit..."

"Aye aye, Captain."

The storm seemed stronger than ever. The wind wailed and thunder rattled, as the ship lurched from side to side.

"We're still taking in water, Captain!" came the desperate cry from one of the crew.

"Well bale it out QUICKER," bawled the Captain, frantically. "Or we will all be DOOMED!"

The mayhem and chaos continued. The Captain barking out orders to the crew and the ship being tossed and buffeted, like a cowboy trying to ride a bucking bronco…

"More men to the PORT side… NOW! Keep BALING it out… FASTER… FASTER…!"

Eventually the sea became more tranquil and the orders became less agitated and frequent.

"We're close to shore, now Captain, if my charts are right."

"They'd better be, bosun," replied the Captain wearily.

"It's a natural harbour here, Captain - much calmer. We should be safe from the gale now…"

"Good work, bosun. You deserve an extra ration of rum this evening. ANCHORS AWAY! We rest here for the night men."

* * *

The crew looked exhausted and relieved. Soon they were all back down below singing and drinking into the night - celebrating their successful mission. They sang songs about treasure and rum and great battles won - even the Captain looked in good spirits.

"More rum, for everyone, cabin girl!" ordered the Captain, almost smiling. "You're still a bit young for a tipple…"

After the cabin girl had seen to the Captain's request, she came over to us and to our surprise gave us some water and biscuits. We thanked her and gobbled them down as we were all starving.

"Take these, you must be freezing." smiled the cabin

girl, returning a few minutes later with some thick blankets. "I'm sure my uncle will let you return to your families. He has an obsession with this treasure, but I do not think he wants to harm you."

We thanked her again. It was a kind gesture to give us the blankets and to give us hope that the Captain would release us, but none of us really believed her. We were now prisoners on board the *Golden Age*, and unless we could be rescued or escape we would be prisoners for a very long time…

Chapter 5

Miracle Monkey

I woke early to the sound of the waves breaking lightly on the shore. It was still dark apart from a narrow shaft of light coming through the port hole. The guards were still snoring loudly. Maybe their night of rum and celebration had given us a chance...

A chance to ESCAPE...

Unfortunately, we were still chained up and the padlock which secured us looked impossible to break – even though Minoo had managed to wriggle out from the chains quite easily during the night.

If only we could ALL wriggle out from our chains like Minoo...

I remembered reading about a 'Miracle Man' called

Houdini who managed to twist himself out of impossible situations in a matter of seconds. We could do with him now I thought.

Minoo had woken up too and was fidgeting with his tail as usual. Suddenly it gave me an idea. Maybe Minoo could help us? Maybe he could be a 'Miracle Monkey'? If we could find the key for the padlock, he might be able to get it and set us all free?

I scanned the room excitedly. It must be somewhere close…

The light wasn't good, but I could see our guards slumped up against a table – sadly, no sign of the keys. Over in the corner there were four more pirates asleep on the floor, but again no keys, only empty bottles of rum.

I was about to give up looking when suddenly I noticed them! There they were, just a few metres away, sitting on top of the treasure chest. I almost let out a cry of delight, but thankfully managed to stop myself. The only problem now was that there was a big hefty pirate asleep - RIGHT next to them. It was no ordinary pirate either - that's right, it was Captain Red himself...

I woke up the others quietly and whispered my escape idea. They all looked excited and gave me the thumbs up, so that was that - the next part was all down to Minoo. Could he rescue the keys from under the nose of the Captain?

I pointed at the keys on the treasure chest and then at our padlock. Minoo jumped up and down excitedly. He knew what he had to do - I think...

Minoo moved quickly and quietly across the cabin floor and climbed carefully up onto the treasure chest. He was just about to gather the keys when the Captain turned over and groaned. Minoo jumped down instantly and hid behind the chest until he thought it was safe to try again. After a few seconds, he climbed up again and carefully lifted the keys from their resting place...

Suddenly the Captain sat up bolt upright and murmured to himself. Either he was having a nightmare or he was awake, in which case we were DONE for... Minoo froze and so did we - praying the Captain was having a nightmare...

After a few agonizing seconds, (which actually seemed like an eternal life time), the Captain grunted, rested his head back on the Treasure chest and started to snore...

We couldn't believe our luck!

Minoo didn't waste any time. He instantly sprang over to us with his prime catch and I welcomed him with a massive hug of congratulations. He really was like a mini Houdini! There were four keys on the ring and hopefully one would free us...

The others watched nervously as I reached down awkwardly to try them. Unfortunately, my arms weren't quite long enough to reach, so I passed them over to Tametoa. The first two keys failed but the third worked perfectly - the lock sprang open! We were free, but not quite yet...

Tametoa hooked the padlock out of the chain and then carefully, and ever so quietly, he unravelled us all until we were all completely FREE...

There was no time to lose. One of the pirates was sure to wake up any second. We had to get off the ship - right NOW! There was no way we could take the treasure at this moment - we would have to come back for it later...

We tiptoed silently past the slumbering pirates and up the timber steps. Soon we were back up on deck, and as we looked out over towards the shore, I could hardly believe my eyes...

Chapter 6

Prickly-Pong Island

It was Prickly-Pong Island…!!

Our magical home for three happy months - before the GHASTLY, giant Prickly-Pong had destroyed it.

The island now looked even more sinister and unwelcoming than when we had been forced to leave it just nine months ago. The once beautiful, vibrant palm trees were now completely withered and dead – overgrown and infested by the malevolent intruders…

It was still almost impossible to believe that the tiny insignificant, cactus-like plants had grown into THIS - horrifying, dark green 'MONSTER-PLANTS' with razor-sharp spikes for teeth. THEY had completely enveloped the island. *Giant rock* and the beach were the only places that were free from its far-reaching tentacles…

I felt shocked and sick with sadness and I'm sure Jana was feeling the same. Then Minoo started to make quiet whimpering noises, which always meant he was nervous or distressed. It was HIS beautiful island that had been destroyed…

"Quick, you two!" whispered Mareva, urgently, pointing down at something. "It's still there!"

We looked down to where Mareva was pointing, and miraculously Nino's battered canoe was still tied to the port side of the *Golden Age*. We climbed back down carefully, using the rope to steady us - not daring to make a sound.

Jana would normally have been panicking and kicking up a fuss, but she knew it was our only hope. We eased ourselves into the canoe silently and set sail. Only one paddle had survived the storm, but we had our Rodu still with us - they would have to make do as make-shift paddles. We were escaping for our lives…

Thankfully, it was only about four hundred metres to

shore and the sea was calm.

"Head for *Giant Rock*," I cried out to Tametoa, who was swimming out in front of us, as the canoe was not big enough for us all. "The one that looks a bit like a volcano…"

As we drew closer to shore, the foul stench of the giant Prickly-Pong hit us.

"What's that disgusting smell…?" gasped Rai, looking like she was about to be sick.

"Don't look at ME…!" replied Nino, defensively. "POOH! It smells like rotten eggs."

"We believe you this time, Nino!" smirked Jana, screwing up her face in disgust. "It's coming from the red slime oozing out of the giant Prickly-Pong. Revolting isn't it?"

"It sure is," replied Nino, pulling a particularly horrible face. "I hope Captain Red ends up slipping in IT!"

Just at that moment we heard the booming voice of a fuming sea Captain echoing across the water.

"FASTER, everyone!" shouted Mareva, nervously, looking back toward the ship. "They're coming after us…"

Now we were paddling as fast as we possibly could, but we were still forty metres from shore! Suddenly we reaslised that something was wrong – the canoe was taking in water…

We were SINKING!

"It must have been damaged in the storm," sighed Nino, desperately.

"Get out now!" cried Mareva, looking towards the shore. "We will swim the rest of the way."

Nino was upset about leaving his canoe, but it was no time to be sentimental with boat-loads of blood-thirsty pirates on our tail.

"Quick!" cried Mareva, taking Minoo on her back. "I can hear their motor boat…"

"The MOTOR BOAT?" shrieked Jana, getting panicky. "They'll be here in no time!"

Luckily for us, we were all strong swimmers and it was only metres to the shore now. Within a matter of seconds we had reached the shallows of the lagoon and were now able to stand up and run.

"Run like you've never run before!" shouted Tametoa anxiously "They're right behind us..."

I didn't dare look back, but I could hear the engine of the motor boat getting closer and closer, and the cursing of Captain Red getting louder and LOUDER...

What were we going to do? There was no way we could outrun them.

We had to find a place to hide and...

QUICKLY ...!!

Chapter 7

The Secret Cave

Suddenly I had an idea...

"Follow me!" I cried out to the others, sprinting towards the massive waterfall, which we had named *Takootu Falls* last year.

As we sped across the sand, Jana reaslised what I was up to and gave me the thumbs up. "Good thinking, Jay."

"Where are we going?" asked, Nino, inquisitively.

"Just follow him!" shouted Jana urgently.

It didn't take us long. Soon we were at the foot of *Takooutu Falls*, with gallons and gallons of water cascading down from *Giant Rock* high above.

"In there!" I shouted to the others, checking behind to make sure the pirates were out of view.

The others looked at me suspiciously.

"In the waterfall?" inquired Rai, doubtfully.

"There's a secret cave behind it," I replied, urgently. Minoo and I discovered it last year. Follow Jana, and keep to the side or you'll get soaked!"

"Where are you going?" inquired Jana, looking confused and concerned, as I turned to head off in the opposite direction.

"I need to distract them away from here," I replied, hurriedly. "I'll join you in a few minutes or so."

"I will come too, Jay," said Nino, bravely."I am fast like you."

"Count me in as well," cried Tametoa, breathlessly.

Jana ordered us all to be careful and disappeared with the others into *Takootu Falls*.

"Follow me!" I shouted, sprinting across the sand towards the forest, so we were now in the full view of Captain Red and his loathsome pirates.

They were still over a few hundred metres away, but I could hear the bellowing voice of Captain Red on the breeze quite clearly. Last year when we'd been playing, Minoo had discovered a tunnel leading into the back of our secret cave, so that's where I was heading, but not until we had put the pirates off the scent.

We continued to sprint away from the cave in the direction of our old tree house. Before long we came to the forest of giant Prickly-Pong.

"Be careful," I warned the others. "The thorns are lethal – they're extremely sharp!"

Cautiously, we dodged in and out of the huge razor-sharp spikes, using our Rodu to help us. One false move and we would be cut to ribbons. Minoo hung on tightly around my neck and soon we were back in the open, climbing up the steep hill towards *Giant Rock* – now taking great care to stay out of sight.

From our vantage point we could see that boatloads of pirates were still coming ashore. Very soon, the whole island would be swarming with them.

Anxiously, I searched for the entrance to the secret tunnel – we needed to get into our hiding place QUICKLY! I couldn't remember the exact spot where it was, as it had been months since we last used it. I was beginning to feel a bit hot and panicky, until Minoo started chattering excitedly and disappeared into a small gap in the rock. Clever Minoo – he'd found it!

"In there," I whispered urgently to the others, taking

one last check that we were safely out of view of any pirates. "Keep crawling and you will come to the cave…"

"There you are," whispered Jana, nervously, as we appeared from the back of the cavern. "We were starting to get worried."

"So were we," I replied, happily. "I couldn't find the tunnel entrance, but luckily Minoo came to the rescue – again!"

"Clever Minoo," smiled Rai, patting him on his head gently.

Minoo squeaked excitedly, then stood on his head and started pulling some extremely silly faces...

"Thank you Jay," whispered Mareva. "It was a great plan and so brave of you all."

"No problem big sis," smiled Nino, looking happy with himself.

"Our pleasure, Mareva," I replied, moving anxiously to the front section of the cave, where I could spy what was happening down on the beach. "I just hope the plan will work…"

We all waited nervously in the dark cavern, not daring to make a sound, even though there was some noise coming from the waterfall, we didn't want to take any chances. It wasn't long before we heard the clamour of angry voices coming from outside.

"SCURVY DOGS!" raged Captain Red. "Where are they, you dim-witted dodo's? They can't be far from here."

"I seen them rushing up the beach towards them big cactus things!" came a shrill pirate voice.

"Well spotted, sailor," replied Captain Red, excitedly. "Soon they will be our prisoners again. After them! Into the forest we go…"

"Well done, Jay. Well done boys." smiled Jana, giving us all a double thumbs up, as the pirate voices became more and more distant. "Your plan seems to have worked."

"Don't sound too surprised, Jana!" I joked, cheerfully. "We boys can come up with the occasional good idea."

"We boys ALWAYS come up with the good ideas - more like!" chuckled Nino, playfully.

Everyone smiled. It was a relief to feel a little more relaxed after the tension of the last half an hour, but we knew we didn't have long. The pirates would be back very, VERY soon...

Chapter 8

Zeo's Gift

Suddenly, Mareva and Tametoa started to have an intense discussion in their own language, so I knew it was about something serious. Eventually Mareva started to speak to us all.

"Thank you Jay, Jana and Minoo, for helping us to escape and getting us to this safe place. Now it is our turn to help you. The only way we can get home and get back Zeo's Treasure is if we get help from Papa and the Radi. Knowing this, Tametoa is going now to Radimatu to tell them where we are."

"But how…?" inquired Jana, looking confused. "It's miles away…"

"He will swim there." replied Mareva, sounding very

composed. "As you already know Tametoa has been the Champion swimmer in Radimatu for the last two years. He is used to swimming long distances."

"But what if the storm blows up again?" cried Jana, anxiously.

"It's too dangerous!" cried Rai, looking very upset.

"Thank you for your concern everyone, but you need not worry." replied Tametoa, calmly. "Swimming is my special gift that Zeo has given me. Now is the time to use it. Now, before the pirates come back…"

I was amazed at the bravery and calmness Tametoa was showing. It reminded me of Takootu last year when things looked really bad for us. He was risking his life for us all.

We all wished him luck and calm waters and I gave him the last three pieces of Grandma's flapjack to eat, which I still had safely hidden in my hoody pocket. He gratefully accepted them and scoffed the lot down in a matter of seconds.

"This will help me keep going," he smiled, as he finished the last few crumbs.

I hoped it would. Radimatu was a long, long, way away – even for a champion swimmer.

Suddenly we heard a noise from outside the cave. It sounded familiar …

We gazed through the fine spray of the waterfall to investigate, and there down by the lagoon was Rai, calling for Poe.

"Rai, get back here!" cried Nino, rushing out to get her. "If the pirates hear you or see you – we're finished."

"No," replied Rai, continuing to whistle. "I don't want Tametoa going on his own."

"That's OK," whispered Mareva, calmly, checking that the coast was clear. "Please continue, Rai, it's a great idea. We will keep watch. This spot behind the rock should be out of view."

We all kept a keen lookout towards the tangled forest of giant Prickly-Pong, while Rai continued to call. We were all praying for a miracle, and after a short while the miracle occurred. A beautiful blue dolphin came spiralling up out of the water - it was Poe!

Rai smiled the biggest smile I'd seen and waved to her special friend. A short while after, Puati arrived too, much to the relief and excitement of Mareva.

"They will both look after you!" cried Rai, happily.

Then she gave Tametoa a huge hug – in fact we all did - and then he dived into the clear blue ocean.

"Keep well away from the *Golden Age*," warned Mareva, waving goodbye. "Let Zeo's strength and wisdom guide you."

Tametoa sped across the blue lagoon as though all our lives depended on it. Poe and Puati swam close by him, jumping and twirling in the air periodically, as though they were telling us not to worry.

We all looked at each other cheerfully. We were all feeling a sudden sense of new optimism. Now there was a chance, a real chance that Tametoa would bring help and we could dream once more of returning safely to Radimatu.

"Quick!" cried Jana, briskly. "Back to the cave before the pirates come back and see us."

She was right. It was only a matter of time before they returned...

Chapter 9

Red's Rant

We weren't back in our secret cave for long before we heard the unmistakable, grumbling tones of Captain Red. We all crept closer to the front of our hideout, so we could hear what was happening below - making sure we were still well hidden by the steady flow of the waterfall. We could see the Captain just a few metres away on the sands below talking to the first mate. He didn't look happy.

"SCURVY DOGS, Marcus!" he barked, waving his cutlass wildly above his head, as he looked hopefully along the shoreline. "Posh and Hogwash! WHERE be they hiding...?"

Suddenly, the Captain stopped still, and then turned

around slowly until he was facing right our way… as though he had just SPOTTED us!

We all ducked down to the ground instantly, praying that he hadn't. He couldn't possibly have seen us from there - could he...? After an agonising moment the Captain looked back towards the forest and continued ranting about us even more.

"DEVIL and DOUBLOONS! Where are those confounded young sprats…?"

"Are you alright Captain, you have cuts all over your face?"

"Course I'm all right, Marcus," snapped the Captain, angrily. "Don't you fuss so. It's just a few scratches from those pesky prickly cactus plants – they be everywhere. I've got thorns all over…"

"I hope he sat on a really BIG one," whispered Nino, with a huge smirk across his face.

All of a sudden I felt a giggle coming on and I just couldn't STOP it… The more I tried, the more it made me want to laugh. Looking at the others, they were feeling exactly the same. But none of us dared to make a noise. One snigger out of place and he would be on to us...

"And that revolting STENCH," continued the Captain, pulling a revolting face. "It be worse than the worst smell on hells earth! What is it?"

"Not sure Captain," replied the first mate. "Think it's coming from them red flowers."

"I thought flowers were supposed to smell GOOD - infuriating young sprats!" bellowed the Captain, walking closer to the waterfall and washing his wounds in the fresh spring water. "They be making fools of us, but we will have the last laugh." The Captain let out a sinister chuckle. "When we be finding them, we shall string them up from them giant cactus plants. That'll teach them a lesson they won't forget!

"Aye aye, Captain," replied the first mate, excitedly. "That it will!"

My strong urge to giggle out loud suddenly evaporated.

That was a lesson we definitely wanted to MISS. It sounded a hundred times more horrid than the worst ever spelling test...

"Keep the men looking, Marcus." ordered the Captain. "They've got to be in there somewhere. I need to check on the ship."

"Aye aye, Captain," replied the first mate, dutifully.

But at that very moment, a large group of pirates suddenly appeared from the giant, tangled forest of Prickly-Pong...

Chapter 10

Devil Island

It was one of the strangest sights I'd ever witnessed. The pirates came careering over the sand, rushing wildly in all directions – crying and cursing as they went.

"DEMONS!" yelled one, looking like he'd just seen a ghost.

"HELP me!" yelled another clutching his bottom, as though it had just been set on fire.

Before long, more and more pirates started to appear on the beach from all angles – all shrieking and howling in pain.

"It's EVIL!" yelled another, his face covered in a zillion cuts. "And THAT smell is ghastly!"

As they drew closer, we could see they were all covered in red weeping gashes from head to toe. They hurried down to the lagoon to bathe their sore wounds in the cool spring water. They looked exhausted.

"WHAT be going on here?" demanded the Captain, impatiently. "Have you found the young sprats?"

"No Captain, sorry," replied a thin, ugly pirate with no teeth. "There be no sign of them…"

"Well then WHAT pray are you all doing back here..?" replied the Captain, looking like he was about to explode with anger.

"We can't stand it no more, Captain," replied the distraught pirate. "The spikes are like daggers – they are tearing us to shreds!"

"And that red slime gets all over you and the smell is REPULSIVE!" added a hefty pirate with dreadlocks, holding his nose and pulling a repulsive face.

"It's a DEVIL island, Captain!" cursed another pirate, hopping around in circles like a madman. "It's not normal…"

"HOSH and POGWASH," cursed the Captain, swishing his sword wildly through the fresh morning air. "You be the ONES that ain't NORMAL..! Pirates from the Golden Age are supposed to be valiant, fearless fighters – not weak, spineless YELLOW-BELLIES!"

The Captain moved in closer to where the pirates had gathered and eye-balled them menacingly.

"FIND those infuriating young sprats within the hour, or I'll be causing you all a lot more damage than those giant cactus plants!"

The Captain swished his giant sword again violently in the direction of the pirates. "GET back into that forest and find them … RIGHT NOW!!"

"Aye, aye Captain!" replied the pirates fearfully, as they started to hurry away.

We couldn't help smiling as they retreated back into the

forest of giant Prickly-Pong like a bunch of naughty school children. But our smiles were nervous smiles. We knew that we could easily be discovered at any minute and if we were, then it would be US that would be facing the fire and fury of the merciless sea Captain...

Chapter 11

Black's Chart

A short while later we noticed three pirates coming into shore in a rowing boat. They looked rather agitated and ran over to the rocks, where the Captain was taking a mid-morning rest by the lagoon.

 "What's the report, bosun." snapped the Captain, getting to his feet. "Will she be fit to sail by noon?"

"Noon, Captain?" replied the bosun, doubtfully.

"Yes NOON - DEAF ears! I want to get off this godforsaken island as soon as possible - we have important business to attend to."

The bosun looked awkwardly back towards the ship.

"She's still taking in water, Captain. There's no way she will be ready by then…"

"SCURVY DOGS, bosun. Then MAKE her ready! We must sail by noon – do you hear me? Get to it!"

"I'll do my best, Captain."

The cabin girl and the bosun rushed off immediately, but the other pirate remained. I didn't realise who he was at first, but then as I gazed through my telescope, I suddenly recognised him. It was the sinister pirate dressed all in black who had shot poor Takootu!

I started to feel really angry and upset and I'm sure Mareva, Nino and Rai were feeling a thousand times worse.

"What does this mean, Captain?" asked the menacing pirate dressed all in black. "The Bandi will not want to wait for their prize? They might start to think you are trying to trick them and going off with the plunder yourself…"

"No need for your worrying, Black." replied Captain

Red, smiling almost apologetically. "We will be sailing by noon – you have my word."

I couldn't believe it. Captain Red being questioned by another pirate – he even seemed a little bit scared of him. Who was he? This ruthless, threatening pirate they called Black, and why did he have such a hold over the Captain?

"How long will it take to get to our rendezvous?" inquired Black, looking distinctly displeased. "Have you still got that chart I gave you?"

"Yes," replied the Captain," retrieving a scroll of paper from his top jacket pocket, like he was trying to impress his teacher. "It be right here."

The Captain unfolded the map carefully and inspected it for a few moments. "I be thinking it will only take us two hours to get there, at most."

"Good work, Captain." Black replied, taking a closer look at the map himself. "I'm sure the Bandi will be very impressed with your work, not to mention very appreciative."

"I be hoping so," smiled the Captain. "After all this toil and hardship."

I tried to get a closer look at the chart using my telescope, but annoyingly the map was too small to see any details.

"It sounds like they're taking the treasure to another island," whispered Jana, anxiously. "What are we going to do?"

"We need to get hold of that map," replied Mareva, calmly.

Mareva was right. If Captain Red was planning to leave at noon, we might never see the treasure again, it would be lost FOREVER!

"But how are we going to get hold of it?" gasped Nino, hopelessly.

"There must be some way," whispered Jana, thoughtfully.

We needed to come up with a plan and quickly or it would be too late. The treasure could be gone in just a few hours time and there was no sign of the Radi to help us...

Chapter 12

Minoo's Mission

We retreated to the back of the cave to discuss our options…

Option one was to try and steal the map.

Option two was to get back on board ship and steal back the treasure.

Option three was to wait for Takootu and the Radi to come.

"I say we try and steal back the treasure," cried Nino, impatiently, trying out another daring attacking move with his Rodu. "It's the only way!"

"It's a very sure way to get hurt and captured," replied Jana, speaking like a parent.

"It's a very brave idea, Nino," replied Mareva, kindly. "But it is too dangerous to try and get aboard the *Golden Age* in daylight. Papa would not want us to put ourselves in danger unless there was no other choice. Getting the map is the best way forward I think."

"If you say so, big sis," replied Nino, putting his Rodu down disappointedly.

"Couldn't Minoo help us get the map?" asked Rai excitedly. "He's so clever at sneaking around."

Minoo suddenly looked over at us, as though he knew we were talking about him.

"That's a great idea," I replied, enthusiastically. "It won't be easy, but if anyone can do it, Minoo can!"

"The map is in the Captain's top pocket though," said Nino, doubtfully. "Surely he will notice?"

Nino was right – it would be almost impossible for Minoo to take it out undetected.

"Not if he takes his jacket off!" cried Jana, excitedly. "As soon as the sun gets high in the sky he will be so hot with that thick black thing on - he's bound to take it off."

"Very good thinking," cried Mareva, eagerly. "Let's just pray that he does – it's our only hope…"

* * *

We gazed out of our secret hideout hoping and praying that the Captain was beginning to feel the heat. According to my watch it was a quarter past eleven. The sun was blazing down now, but still the Captain made no move to take off his thick black jacket.

"We're running out of time!" whispered Jana, nervously to the others. "The Captain is hoping to set sail at midday – that's only 45 minutes from now..."

"Yeah - it must be baking out there by now," whispered Nino. "What's wrong with the guy? Take it off!"

"He's cold blooded," – quipped Jana. "Like a vampire..!"

Nino started to snigger at Jana's remark, but then just at that moment - it happened! The Captain stood up slowly, wiped his brow with the back of his left hand and took off his fancy pirate jacket - laying it carefully down on the rocks.

We were in business…

Minoo was all ready for action. I had already explained to him what he had to do. I think he understood, but to be honest I wasn't completely sure. (I had used a piece of old screwed up paper I had found in my pocket to pretend it was the map.) We would find out soon enough if he had understood. I gave him a special cuddle and the others all wished him well.

"Be ever so careful, Minoo," I whispered after him.

Minoo let out a playful cry, then nipped through the waterfall and scurried down towards the lagoon. As soon as Minoo was out in the open he crept low over the rocks like a predator about to sneak up on its prey.

The Captain was talking with the first mate who had just returned from the tangled forest of Prickly-Pong. He had cuts all over his face and didn't look a happy pirate. The Captain wasn't looking a happy pirate either

- he kept cursing and looking out towards his ship impatiently.

Suddenly we noticed a small boat coming towards shore. It looked like the bosun and the cabin girl again – no doubt with important news about the ship's repairs. It was almost too good to be true - this was the perfect distraction! Minoo seized his opportunity. Hastily he skulked over to where the Captain's black jacket was laying and started to search carefully through the pockets…

"Quick Minoo," I whispered, nervously, "Find it and get out of there!"

But Minoo's search had hardly got started when all of a sudden things started to go horribly wrong. Captain Red must have noticed him out of the corner of his eye and suddenly he turned around abruptly, his sword drawn for battle.

"Get away - you PESKY monkey! SHOO!"

Minoo didn't need a second invitation and sped away swiftly over the sand.

"That's no ordinary monkey, Captain!" cried the first mate urgently. "It belongs to them kids."

"Maybe you be right, Marcus," replied the Captain, angrily. "Quick then - get after him you SLOW-COACH. He will lead us to the young sprats!"

The first mate gave chase immediately and soon Minoo was fleeing for his life...

"Run Minoo - RUN!" I cried out anxiously, making sure my voice was no more than a murmur.

Jana and the others looked scared.

"Please let him be OK" whispered Rai, apprehensively. "I wish I hadn't suggested him going now..."

Chapter 13

Good News and Bad

Thankfully Minoo was a lot quicker and nippier across the sand than most adults and he sped away from the first mate quite easily. What was more, he didn't run back to the cave and give us all away. Instead he ran back towards the tangled forest of giant Prickly-Pong just like we had done earlier that morning.

"Clever Minoo", cried Nino, quietly. "What a brilliant monkey you are!"

"I hope he will get back to us OK," said Rai, still looking very anxious.

"I'm sure he will," I replied, just praying that he wouldn't run into any murderous pirates on his route back to us. "He'll be here with us soon, Rai. Don't worry…"

"What are we going to do NOW about the map?" sighed Jana, despondently. "The ship will probably be sailing in half an hour and we will still have NO idea where they will be taking the treasure!"

She was right. Time was ticking away rapidly. We needed to get hold of the map quickly but HOW…?

We all looked back out towards the beach, fearing the worst, but suddenly we got an unexpected surprise that immediately lifted our spirits. The bosun and the cabin girl were moving slowly up the beach towards the Captain, but they weren't alone. Just behind them was a gang of pirates who were carrying something that seemed extremely heavy - it was the TREASURE!

"What's going on?" demanded the Captain, angrily. "It's almost midday! What are you doing bringing the booty ashore?"

"It's no good, Captain." replied the bosun, timidly. "We need more time to repair her."

"MORE TIME?" raged the Captain. "MORE TIME…! Posh and Hogwash! I said noon, bosun – we be 12 hours behind schedule already."

"S...S.. Sorry, Captain, but she's still taking in water," continued the bosun, looking all hot and bothered. "We're going to have to work on her all day and try to get her seaworthy by sunset, so we can sail at sun-rise tomorrow."

"TOMORROW?" exploded the Captain, looking like he wanted to decapitate the bosun with one swish of his cutlass.

"She's more damaged than we thought, Uncle." explained the cabin girl. "We were lucky she didn't go down last night with US on board AND the treasure."

"All right," barked the Captain, furiously. "I get the message! Tomorrow at dawn it is."

"But what about our urgent rendezvous, Captain?" demanded Black, coldly.

"Did you not hear the bosun, man?" replied the Captain, irritably. "We have NO ship to sail us! What else can we be doing? We be marooned on this godforsaken island until tomorrow…"

"Where shall we put the treasure, Captain?" asked one of the pirate's, sheepishly.

"Leave it here for now." snapped the Captain, still seething with anger. "Later we can take it up to that tree house we saw –best we make that our camp for the night..."

While this was very bad news for the Captain – it was very BRILLIANT news for us!

The longer the pirates had to stay on the island, the longer there was for help to arrive, and the more time we had to get hold of the map or even rescue back the treasure.

But suddenly our attention turned to Minoo. He still hadn't arrived back and I was starting to feel concerned - in fact we all were. We waited nervously at the back of the cave. The time seemed to pass very slowly...

 "Minoo better be all right," whispered Rai, anxiously. "If anything has happened to him, I'll never forgive myself..."

"He'll be here soon, Rai," I said, trying to offer her a little comfort, even though I was beginning to feel extremely anxious myself. "He's probably going the long way around to put them off the scent. He knows this island better than any of us."

"Yes I'm sure he'll be here soon," added Mareva, reassuringly."He's cleverer than all those pirates put together!"

We all smiled and hoped Mareva was right...

Chapter 14

Trapped

We waited, and we waited and we waited some more, but still there was NO sign of Minoo.

"I'm going out there!" I whispered, anxiously as I moved towards the secret passageway at the back of the cave. "Something must have happened to him..."

"You can't go on your own Jay," said Mareva, decisively. "If Minoo is trapped or captured – you will need our help..."

After a quick discussion it was decided that Mareva and Nino would come with me, but Rai and Jana would stay behind in the cave just in case Minoo came back from across the sand. They wished us good luck and we wriggled up the secret passageway and out onto the

217

mountainside.

We kept VERY low to the ground and looked all around us apprehensively. If the pirates spotted us so close to our secret cave we were all TOAST! We found a safe viewpoint up the hillside and from there I scanned all around - my eye firmly pressed to my telescope...

I could see pirates below cursing in pain as they continued to explore the tangled forest of giant Prickly-Pong. I could see Captain Red on the beach sitting on the treasure chest nursing his wounds. I could see the *Golden Age* at anchor off the shore, with its Jolly Rodger fluttering in the breeze...

But there was NO sign of MINOO.

"Where are you..?" I said to myself, beginning to feel REALLY scared.

Suddenly there was a noise.

"Did you hear something, Mareva?"

Mareva shock her head. "No, sorry Jay."

"I heard something," whispered Nino, eagerly. "It sounded like it was coming from up above..."

Suddenly I heard the sound again – we all heard it this time. It sounded like... WHIMPERING... I knew that sound! It was MINOO – it had to be and he sounded like he was in trouble... BIG... BIG trouble!

We scrambled swiftly, but softly up the trail towards the summit of *Giant Rock*, the one I used to scale with Minoo last year almost every day. Every step we took, we looked about ourselves nervously - eyes and ears open – senses on high alert. As we drew closer we suddenly heard voices...

PIRATE voices!

We hit the ground instantly and crept ever so slowly and ever so silently, until we could just see over the ridge ahead...

My worst fears were confirmed. There was Minoo perched high up on a ledge on the edge of the cliff whimpering anxiously. He couldn't climb up any higher – it was a sheer face of rock and the path below was blocked by three hefty pirates...

He was TRAPPED!!

It was just like my daydream in class earlier in the year, but this time it was Minoo on his OWN on the edge of the cliff escaping from pirates, and this time it was definitely NO daydream - it was for REAL!

What were we going to do…?

My heart raced and so did my brain. We had to do something to help - but WHAT…?

"Go up and get him!" snarled a huge bald headed pirate with a scar across his cheek.

"Are you CRAZY, man?" replied a tall, stocky looking pirate with no teeth. "He's on the edge of the blasted CLIFF! And you knows I don't like heights…"

"Stop moaning, chicken-legs," replied the scar-faced pirate. "The first mate says there'll be a reward if we catch him. They want to use the monkey as a ransom to get them kids."

"You goes up there then, if you're so keen…"

The scar-faced pirate scowled and didn't budge from his spot.

"I know how to get him down," shouted a dumpy, wild looking pirate. "Watch this!"

He picked up a few large rocks from the ground and started hurling them towards poor defenceless Minoo.

"These will bring him to us soon enough!"

The first rock flew harmlessly over the cliff, but the second was right on TARGET...

Minoo had to jump acrobatically to his right in order to dodge it, and just managed to avoid falling headlong over the cliff.

"IDIOT!" cried the scar-faced pirate, angrily. "We want to scare him back down here NOT smash him into the blasted OCEAN."

I couldn't bear to watch anymore. If we waited any longer one of those rocks would hit Minoo clean off the CLIFF! I looked over at Mareva and I could tell she was thinking the same thing – as was Nino, who had his

Rodu primed for an attack...

Mareva led the charge as we caught all three pirates by surprise.

"Stay right by me!" ordered Mareva, as she swung her Rodu with great venom into her first victim, using one of her special 'High-Cross' moves.

"AHHHHHHH…!" came the piercing cry, as the dumpy wild looking pirate got knocked over the edge and into the ocean below.

"Bulls-eye," cried Nino, excitedly. "Great move - big sis!"

I was glad to see the back of that particular pirate, but there were still two more to worry about and their weapons were now drawn and ready for the fight…

"Capture them!" shouted the scar-faced pirate launching a frenzied attack on Mareva with his razor-sharp cutlass. "The reward will be ours!"

"Now you're talking!" laughed the toothless pirate, menacingly as he joined in the attack, dagger drawn. "We might get some of them priceless gold Doubloons as a prize…!"

"We need to be QUICK!" shouted Mareva, anxiously, as she defended herself desperately against the two mercenary pirates.

"Everyone on the island will have heard THAT cry. They will all be up here in a matter of minutes!"

Mareva was right. The whole place was going to be swarming with pirates in the next few moments, so there was no time to lose.

But poor Mareva was now in trouble – she looked tired and possibly even injured. The pirates were fighting hard and Mareva was having to retreat backwards - inching closer and closer towards the EDGE of the cliff…   We had to do something… and quickly…!

"Take THAT!" bellowed Nino, as he smashed his Rodu

across the back of the scar-faced pirate.

"And THAT!" I cried, crashing my Rodu hard into the side of the tall, stocky toothless pirate.

Both pirates turned to face us - they were FUMING!

"These two small fry won't take us long," laughed the scar-faced pirate, thrusting his cutlass towards us in a vicious attack.

Suddenly WE were the ones having to defend ourselves to stay alive! Now we were the ones retreating, inching closer and closer to the EDGE of the cliff... Things weren't looking good at all...

But just at that moment Minoo appeared from nowhere. He leaped courageously onto the back of the scar-faced pirate and hung onto his neck tightly like a limpet – upsetting his aim and composure.

"Get off me – you bothersome ape!" cursed the scar-faced pirate, as he grappled Minoo off and flung him to the ground.

Minoo looked shaken, but thankfully he was all right

and the distraction was just what we needed. Mareva had recovered. She had got her second wind and was back on FULL attack mode once more. Swishing and lashing her Rodu skillfully through the air at tremendous speed…

It was too much for our blood-thirsty opponents. Within a matter of seconds both the pirates were sent FLYING over the cliff edge, spiralling downwards to their watery doom.

"AHHHHHHHHHHHHHHH………"

"NOOOOOOOOOOOO………"

"Great work, big-sis!" cried Nino, triumphantly.

"QUICK!" replied Mareva, nervously looking back down the steep hillside. "We need to go. The rest of them will be up here any second..."

Mareva was dead right. We had to move now and move quickly. I grabbed hold of Minoo tightly and we were off! I could feel his heart beating faster than ever, but thank goodness he was safe now - at least for the time being...

We ran as fast as we had ever run before. Back down the steep trail – jumping over boulders and small streams of spring water as we went.

Soon we were by the entrance to the secret passageway. We could hear agitated pirate voices coming from below and we knew that they would be up here any second. We paused and double-checked the coast was clear before disappearing inside.

As we crawled breathlessly through the tunnel, we just hoped and prayed that we hadn't been spotted…

Chapter 15

Fingers Crossed

"There you are!" cried Jana, giving us all an emotional embrace. "We've been worried sick…"

"Yes we have," agreed Rai tearfully, giving Minoo the biggest hug of his life. "I'm so happy you are all safe."

"So are we!" smiled Nino, cheerily.

"We're not safe YET," whispered Mareva, anxiously. "There are probably twenty or more pirates out there right now - snooping around searching for us. We must pray they don't discover the secret tunnel – if they do we must all be ready to make a run for it along the beach…"

We all nodded solemnly and waited nervously at the

back of the cave, listening intently for any sound of the pirates coming - fingers firmly crossed.

The wait was agonising...

We were all set and ready to sprint away at the slightest hostile sound. Jana looked terrified and was chewing her nails uneasily. My nerves felt like they did on sports day at the start of a race, waiting for the gun to go off but THIS was a zillion times worse...

What would they do with us if they caught us..?

Hang us upside-down from the giant Prickly-Pong to die in the heat...?

Make us walk the plank off the *Golden Age*...

Push us off the top of *Giant Rock*...

Feed us to the ravenous sharks...

Or just slit our throats...

Whatever they decided to do to us, it was going to be BAD, but worse still was the fact that we would have failed. Zeo's Treasure would be lost and theirs for ever...

We waited and we waited for what seemed like hours, but thankfully we heard nothing. This was too good to be true! Were we actually safe...? Had they missed the secret tunnel...?

All of a sudden we heard angry voices, but it was coming from the beach not the secret passageway. We moved quietly to the front of the cave and could hear Captain Red having another of his furious rants and his pirates were once more on the receiving end...

"DEVIL AND DOUBLOONS! They can't just have disappeared off the cliff, you MORONS! They must have escaped and be hiding some place in the forest or on the mountain top. Find them and find them QUICKLY!"

The pirates looked reluctant to go back into the forest again and get torn to shreds, but the Captain was in no mood for compromise.

"SCURVY DOGS! What you be waiting for? Now I say - you snivelling yellow-bellies! What's more I'll give ten gold Doubloons for any man that finds them young sprats. BUT if I do hear that any man is not pulling his weight, I will string him up on them monster cactus plants in the hot burning sun. Understood...??? "

The Captain glared into the eyes of his crew and waved his cutlass violently above his head. I think the crew understood him all right, and within seconds they were moving away sheepishly towards the forest.

As they left, we all let out a huge sigh of relief. Somehow the pirates had missed the entrance to the tunnel, but it was only a temporary reprieve – they would now be searching all day until they found us. And now that there was a reward of ten gold Doubloons on our heads they would be searching even harder.

We spent the whole afternoon on tenterhooks. Any second the pirates could discover us and we would have to flee over the beach for our LIVES... As we waited, we talked about brave Tametoa. Was he safe? Had he managed to swim all the way to Radimatu yet? Was help coming?

"He should be there by now," said Nino, hopefully.

"Yes - Papa could be on his way to save us!" cried Rai, optimistically.

"Not yet," replied Mareva. "Tametoa is a fast swimmer, but it is a long way even for him. Hopefully he will arrive in the next hour or so, but it will be too dark by then for Papa and the Radi to set sail."

We all let out a groan of disappointment.

"But I am sure Papa will set sail first thing tomorrow…" continued Mareva, confidently.

"But tomorrow's going to be too late," sighed Jana sounding very upset. "The *Golden Age* is sailing at DAWN!"

Jana was right. If the *Golden Age* did set sail Zeo's Treasure would be lost forever, unless we could get hold of that special chart...

"We need to get hold of that map!" I cried, desperately. "Somehow – don't ask me how - we need to sneak up on the pirates and steal it out of Captain's Red top pocket. It's the only way."

"It's the only way to get CAPTURED again," sighed Jana, dismissively. "Look what happened to poor Minoo."

"Jay is right," said Mareva, calmly. "Yes, it might be very dangerous, but it is our only hope. We must get hold of that chart so we know where the Captain is taking the treasure. It's our last chance."

After a brief discussion we all agreed it was our last and only chance and started to formulate a plan immediately. We knew what we HAD to do – that was the easy part. How we were actually going to succeed in doing it was going to be a lot lot LOT more difficult...

But at least we had 'Miracle Minoo' back safe and well to help us.

Chapter 16

Dawn Attack

We woke an hour before dawn. I had set an alarm on my watch so we would be up bright and early, but we didn't need it. Minoo was jumping on my head squealing and looked extremely agitated.

Something was wrong and it didn't take us long to work out what it was - the earth was moving! Yes MOVING! It wasn't a nightmare. There was a faint rumbling sound coming from all around us. Petrified, we ran outside onto the sand and sprinted up the beach in the eerie moonlight.

Soon we were at the fringes of the forest, and as we looked back we noticed an orange glow coming from the top of *Giant Rock*, and there was some white smoke billowing out of it. It looked just like a volcano! A volcano about to ERUPT...

"I thought you said it wasn't active?" whispered Nino, looking scared out of his wits.

"We didn't think it WAS!" I replied, my heart racing.

"Quick," whispered Mareva urgently. "We have even less time now to get the map and the treasure."

The pirates had made camp at our old tree-house, so that's where we were heading for. The forest looked even more sinister in the moonlight, but at least it helped us to see where we were going. Cautiously, we moved our way through the entangled maze of giant Prickly-Pong, taking great care to avoid the razor-sharp thorns and repulsive goo oozing out from the blood red flowers. We used our Rodu to pin back the spiky thorns and clear a safe way through.

"There he is," whispered Nino, who was at the front of the group with me and Minoo. We hid in the undergrowth and waited nervously.

The Captain was sleeping in the bottom hammock, with his jacket draped over him like a blanket. He appeared to be sleeping soundly, judging by the loud snoring we could hear.

Minoo knew what to do and was off like a whippet. Within seconds he was right by the Captain's side, carefully searching through the pockets. Almost immediately he appeared to have found something and bounded back to us eagerly.

"This looks like it!" I whispered, excitedly handing over the map to Mareva.

"Great work, Minoo," whispered Mareva, affectionately. "This could be so important to Papa and our people! You keep it, please Jay. You have deep pockets to keep it safe."

I took the map back from Mareva and pushed it right down into my pocket as far as it would go. I knew how vital it might be for Takootu and the Radi. The next part of our plan was going to be even more difficult and dangerous, but we didn't have time to worry about it – we had to act now.

"Ready?" inquired Mareva, looking over to us all, with a Radi warrior glint in her eyes.

"Ready," we all whispered back to her, giving her the thumbs up.

The Treasure chest was only a few metres away from the Captain, but it was surrounded by more than a dozen slumbering pirates. We tip-toed through them, as carefully and as quietly as we could. One foot out of place and we were done for. It was like walking through a mine field and it was going to be ten times harder on the way back carrying the treasure.

Amazingly, we managed to get through unscathed, and were just about to lift the heavy chest when disaster struck…

All of a sudden, the ground started to shudder violently and the rumbling from *Giant Rock* seemed to be getting louder and LOUDER…

The pirates woke up instantly and we were stuck right in the middle of them… SURROUNDED!

"Well, well, well…gentlemen," mocked the Captain, springing to his feet, and circling us triumphantly. "Look what we've caught ourselves here!? A bountiful net full of juicy young sprats. Perfect food for feeding to the SHARKS!!"

The pirates, who were now all awake, cheered excitedly, but we had no intention of being fed to any sharks. We launched into battle with our Rodu firing on all cylinders and managed to land a few good blows.

"Take that!" shouted Nino, looking pleased that he was able to use another of his special moves.

Mareva fought like a true Radi warrior, taking out half a dozen pirates or more with lighting quick blows, but sadly it was all to no avail. We were heavily outnumbered and within a minute or two the battle was lost and we had no other choice but to surrender. Defeated, we all huddled together nervously – Minoo hanging on tight around my neck. Dawn was almost up and so was our last chance of rescuing the treasure…

"Secure them, men!" smirked Captain Red, jubilantly. "We will drop them overboard for the sharks, one by one, on the way to our important rendezvous…"

All of a sudden, the rumbling from *Giant Rock* became

even louder and the intense orange glow became even brighter. Huge plumes of white smoke started pouring from the top...

"The rock's on FIRE!" screamed a terrified pirate.

"That's no ordinary rock – you bird-brain!" shouted the Captain. "It's a LIVE VOLCANO and it's about to BLOW!! Abandon Island! RUN for the ship! And don't forget them young sprats or the treasure!"

Chapter 17

Fire and Fury

Within ten terrifying minutes, we were all aboard the *Golden Age* – reluctant captors of Captain Red once more. We looked back towards Prickly-Pong Island and could hardly believe what we could see...

Giant Rock was spitting fire like a fuming dragon in an adventure movie. Streams of blood-red larva were pouring down *Takootu Falls* turning it into a waterfall of fire. Our once beautiful island was erupting before our very eyes!

Minoo let out a distressing whimper and held on to me more tightly than ever. His island hadn't had much luck in the past year – first the giant Prickly-Pong and now THIS. It was burning like an inferno – poor Minoo.

"I knew that island be bad news the minute I do set foot on her!" yelled Captain Red, looking wilder than ever against the magenta sky. "Good riddance I say!"

"She's ready to sail, Captain," reported the bosun, respectfully.

"Good work, sailor, ANCHORS AWAY!" cried the Captain, cheerfully. "You knows our destination. Just make sure you keeps an eye out for them confounded rocks."

"Aye aye, Captain," replied the bosun, returning to his post.

"Listen up, crew," continued the Captain, excitedly.

"We should be at our rendezvous, in just a few hours and this very evening we be having the biggest party EVER to celebrate!"

The pirates laughed and cheered happily.

"Double rum rations for everyone!" continued the Captain, jubilantly. "And no chores or scrubbing the deck for this voyage - the young sprats will be doing that - until we do decide to drop them overboard to the SHARKS…"

The pirates cheered again heartily and started to sing old mariner songs of victories, rum and treasure. We huddled close together, tired and hungry. Suddenly we felt very alone and desperate – all our usual optimism was gone. Yesterday was meant to be our special day - the day we opened the Museum at Radimatu, with our family and Takootu and all the wonderful, friendly Radi villagers watching.

Would we ever see any of them again..?

Soon we would be far out at sea in some far-away waters, with a band of murderous pirates, with no hope of Takootu and the Radi ever finding us or Zeo's Treasure, EVER again…

Chapter 18

Bandi Bombshell

"Ships ahoy, Captain!" cried a young-looking pirate, high up in the crow's nest. "Coming from the east!"

We gazed nervously towards the horizon. The sun was dazzling us, still low in the early morning sky. Suddenly, we saw them - dozens and dozens of fishing boats and battle canoes sailing towards us at great speed! Tametoa must have made it. The Radi were coming to SAVE us!

"DEVIL and DOUBLOONS!" cursed the Captain, looking shocked and shaken. "They be MASSES of them! Battle stations! Prime the cannons! Hoist the main sail – we will try and outrun them!"

"Aye aye, Captain," replied the first mate, springing

into action at once.

"I knew Papa would come to save us!" beamed Rai, ecstatically.

"Now he will sort out Captain Red and his PATHETIC pirates once and for all!" cried Nino, excitedly.

"Can you see him, Jay?" asked Rai, looking more concerned.

While the pirates were carrying out their new orders, I gazed through my telescope nervously, scanning the horizon to the east for Takootu. I could see fishing boats full of villagers, battle canoes full of Radi warriors, but there was no sign of Takootu or the *Captain Cook*...

"Sorry, Rai," I replied, sadly. "I can't see him."

"He is there with them," replied Rai, calmly. "I know he is."

No one said anything. We were all secretly praying that Rai's sixth sense was as reliable as always; to think otherwise was just too upsetting to contemplate.

"They're gaining on us, Captain!" cried the first mate, anxiously, peering through his spyglass.

"POSH and HOGWASH!" cursed the Captain, looking out to sea anxiously. "Them battle canoes are moving faster than what I thought. Prime the cannons! Prepare to do BATTLE! Fight for each other and die for each other..."

The fleet of Radi craft was inching closer and closer and with it our spirits were getting brighter and brighter. Soon the Radi warriors would be with us - they would capture the *Golden Age* and we would all be saved AND the Treasure!

"Ships ahoy, Captain!" came another cry from the crow's nest. "Three ships to the south - flying the Skull and Crossbones..!"

"The BANDI!" cried the Captain, laughing gleefully. "What perfect timing. Now the tables have turned. Now we will be able to BLOW the Radi scum clean out of the water!"

"I told you they'd be nervous about the treasure," added Black, in a smug and superior manner. "They probably think you are trying to escape with it yourselves..."

"Stuff and nonsense," replied the Captain, indignantly. "I be a man of my word."

Our hearts sank again – this was not the news we wanted to hear. The three Bandi ships approaching from the south, were similar to the *Golden Age*, but looked even grander and more intimidating with twice as many cannons. Soon the brave Radi warriors and villagers would be feeling the full force of their fire power.

Things were looking bad for us again - REALLY bad...

I scanned the horizon for Takootu once more, but there was still no sign of him. I started to feel sick with guilt. If I hadn't found Zeo's Treasure in the first place, none of this would be happening. The Radi would not be putting their lives in grave danger and Takootu would be alive and well. It was ALL my fault.

Chapter 19

Sinking Feeling

All of a sudden, we heard loud shouts and voices coming from below.

"She's taking in water!" cried the bosun, frantically, rushing across the deck towards the Captain.

"SCURVY DOGS!" cursed the Captain, angrily. "I thought you said SHE be fixed?"

"Sorry Captain," replied the bosun anxiously. "I thought she was mended, good and proper, but the patch hasn't held – the water's gushing in!"

"Well sort it, bosun and be quick about it!" bellowed the Captain, heatedly. "All hands below!"

"It's too late for that Captain," cried the first mate desperately. "I've just seen it with my own eyes – the lower deck is completely submerged! The Treasure is lost – we can't reach it. Abandon ship - abandon ship!"

"DEVIL and DOUBLOONS!" cursed the Captain, going into a frenzy. "I give the orders around here, Marcus. All hands below - NOW – that is an order! The treasure MUST be saved at all costs - ALL hands below - THIS INSTANT!!"

"Aye aye, Captain" replied his first mate, standing awkwardly by the Captain's side like a loyal dog.

But the other pirates weren't listening to the Captain, or if they were, they just chose to ignore him. Some were getting into rowing boats and others were jumping straight off the ship into the choppy waters below…

"Yellow-bellied, treacherous, TRAITORS!" screamed the Captain, desperately. "Come back, here NOW! MUTINY! That is an order…"

Still the pirates continued to flee the sinking ship.

"Uncle - it's no good," pleaded the cabin girl, about to leap over the side. "She's going down FAST – jump while you still have the chance!"

"Not you as well, Kat!" sighed the Captain, dejectedly. "Be off with you girl – go now and be safe."

"The Bandi will not take kindly to their treasure going down." sneered Black, spitefully. "What are you going to do now, Captain..?"

The Captain said nothing. He looked helpless, almost desperate but he wasn't finished. Suddenly he started swishing his cutlass wildly above his head and went into a menacing rage…

"I'll tell you what I be going to do – Mr WHINGY-WHINY – backbiting Black! I'm going to rescue the booty right NOW - this instant - and you're going to help me do it!"

"But what about the ship...?" replied the black pirate anxiously. "She's going under…?"

"A YELLOW-BELLY too - are we?" sneered the

Captain. "You should be more fearful of the Bandi, if we don't bring them their treasure, they will have our guts for garters! We go together - now! And you three guards too - while there's still time..."

 "What about the young sprats?" asked one of the three pirates guarding us.

"Bring them with you – right away!" ordered the Captain, slyly. "They can accompany us down below - they say it be THEIR treasure after all..."

The Captain laughed out loud and pushed the black pirate towards the steps leading to the lower deck - with his cutlass pressed hard at his back.

"After you, yellow-belly," sneered the Captain, as they disappeared below.

We glanced at each other nervously... There was no way we wanted to do down below with them. Even if the treasure was still there, it would be impossible to rescue – we would all DROWN...

"Quick!" cried Mareva, courageously pulling her Rodu

out from the sling across her back and launching a surprise attack on our guards. "Fight like you've never fought before!"

Thankfully, in the panic, our guards hadn't had time to tie us up or take our weapons.

"Leave them to me, big sis!" cried Nino, cheerfully joining in the attack.

Within seconds we were all locked into battle. We were swinging and swishing our Rodu and trying to remember all the skills that Takootu had taught us the year before. Then it had been fighting for fun, but now we were fighting for our LIVES...

The pirates looked ruthless and mean and we had to use all our guile to dodge their swords as they launched a ferocious attack. Thankfully our defence moves were just managing to hold them, but we couldn't hold them off for much longer...

Time was running out. Not only did we have the bloodthirsty pirates to worry about – the *Golden Age* was SINKING... and sinking...FAST!

"We need to get off this ship – now!" cried Mareva desperately, as she knocked one of the pirates to the floor. "Move closer to the side. I will shield you - get ready to jump…"

"No way!" cried Jana, hysterically. "I can't jump down there. You know I don't like heights or sharks…"

"Come on, Jana!" I cried, pulling her towards the side. "It's not that far down now. We will all jump over together - it's our only chance..."

"When you hit the water - swim away from the ship!" cried Mareva, breathlessly, as she repelled another attack. "And use your Rodu to help you float."

The situation was desperate. We couldn't bear the thought of leaving Zeo's Treasure behind, but we had no choice…

"Now!" cried Mareeva, decisively, as she rushed to the edge to join us.

Jana didn't put up a fight and within a matter of seconds, we were all plunging at high-speed towards the ocean! Mareeva close to Jana, Nino next to Rai and Minoo gripping tightly round my neck like a limpet…

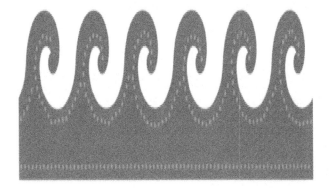

Chapter 20

HELP!

It was like the scariest ride at the water park, but much, much worse. This was for real – it was life and death..! We hit the water with a huge SPLASH! The water wasn't as cold as I'd expected, but the waves were WHOPPERS…

We'd never swum in deep water like this before, but thankfully we still had our Rodu. We held them out in front of us, like Mareva had told us to do, and they acted just like a float – the wood was surprisingly buoyant.

The sea was swarming with pirates cursing and crying for help. Some looked like they couldn't swim, but most of them were safely aboard their rowing boats.

"Swim away from the ship!" cried Mareva,

desperately. "Or we'll get sucked under…"

We understood what Mareva was worried about, and managed to summon up enough strength to get a few metres away. The lower deck of the *Golden Age* was almost completely submerged now – I couldn't believe how fast the ship was sinking.

"Keep treading water, everyone!" shouted, Mareva, anxiously. "The Radi will be here soon to rescue us."

But the Radi had their own problems to deal with, as they were now in the middle of a perilous sea battle. We could hear the rumble of cannon fire in the distance which meant the Bandi ships must have opened fire. We hoped and prayed the brave Radi villagers and warriors would survive. If they were defeated by the Bandi all hope of rescue would be gone.

All of a sudden, Rai started whistling loudly. She was calling for Poe. Then Mareva started to call for Puati. If ever we needed a friendly dolphin around to help us it was NOW! They continued calling for a few minutes, but sadly there was no sign of Poe or Puati.

With the sound of cannons blasting, pirates crying and waves crashing, it was unlikely they could hear their calls. We just had to accept it - we were on our own, unless the Radi could somehow rescue us.

Minutes passed and still there was no sign of any help. We were beginning to feel tired and exhausted, especially Jana who wasn't the strongest swimmer. Mareva had noticed she was struggling and put a comforting arm around her to help keep her above water.

The rest of us gripped on to our Rodu tightly. Minoo was sitting on my shoulders, chattering to himself and making nervous whimpering noises – no doubt wishing he was high up in his favourite palm tree back home in Zeo. We continued to tread water as best we could, but our arms and legs were beginning to feel like jelly – we couldn't hold out much longer...

"Help!" cried Mareva, desperately, looking over towards the Radi battle canoes which were getting closer and closer. "Help us!!"

But there was no reply.

Soon we were all crying frantically for help.

"HELP…!"

"HELP…!"

"HELP…!"

Maybe, just maybe, our voices would carry, and someone would come for us. We just hoped they would get to us in time…

Chapter 21

Radi Rescue

We had started to give up hope of ever being rescued when all of a sudden we heard a loud voice coming over the water. We looked around hopefully, but all we could see were plumes of black smoke coming from the Bandi canons.

A few seconds passed and then we heard the same voice again - it sounded familiar...

"Mareva! Hang on – we're coming for you..."

We twisted around eagerly and this time we saw HIM! There was Tametoa leaning out of the *Captain Cook* waving at us all excitedly.

"Tametoa!" we all cried with joy and amazement.

We could hardly believe it - brave Tametoa had swum all the way back to Radimatu and now he was here to save us! But there was more excitement and surprises to come, for behind Tametoa at the helm, we noticed another VERY familiar face…

It was Takootu with his beaming smile – it was TAKOOTU!

"Papa!" cried Rai, jubilantly. "I knew you would come to save us."

Takootu steered the boat in close, and one by one, they hauled us up safely onto the *Captain Cook*. Takootu looked injured. He had a large bandage wrapped around his left arm, but he was ALIVE! He was ALIVE!

I'd never been so pleased in all my life to see someone and looking at the others neither had they. Smiles of happiness and relief were written all over our faces – we started to laugh and cry all at the same time. Takootu looked equally pleased to see us and especially Mareva, Nino and Rai who he hugged for what seemed like an eternity.

"Never be doing that again," he whispered, with tears in his eyes. "You is all being too precious to me."

"Promise, Papa," replied Rai affectionately, still hugging Takootu tightly.

"What about the treasure?" gasped Tametoa, urgently.

"It was with us in the ship..." replied Mareva, looking sadly towards the *Golden Age*, which was now almost completely under water. The main mast was still just visible with the Skull and Crossbones fluttering forlornly in the breeze.

"It was on the lower deck, Papa – which was completely submerged, according to the first mate." continued Mareva, looking devastated. "The last thing we saw was Captain Red going down to try and rescue it, but it sounded an impossible task."

"I see," replied Takootu, thoughtfully.

"I hope he drowns down there!" cried Nino, angrily. "And especially that despicable Black pirate with him."

There was no sign of the Captain or Black in the water.

There was a very good chance that they had both perished trying to rescue the treasure, but not one of us knew for sure.

"Shall I dive down, Papa?" asked Tametoa, courageously. "If I take some warriors with me, we might be able retrieve it?"

"NO, Tametoa," replied Takootu firmly. "It is much too dangerous to be trying such a thing. The treasure will have to wait for another time. It is causing enough heartache already these past days. We set sail for home right now - while we can - before more Radi people is getting hurt."

Takootu was right to be alarmed. The three Bandi galleons were almost upon us.

"Soon we is being in range of their cannons," cried Takootu, anxiously. "They is too many and too strong – we is sailing home now to Radimatu - to live and fight another day."

Takootu gave the signal to the Radi fleet, who raised their Rodu in solidarity, and we set off immediately back to Radimatu. The Bandi galleons were formidable fighting machines and they immediately gave chase, firing volley after volley from their thundering cannons.

Maybe they thought we were escaping with the treasure, or maybe they just wanted to teach us a lesson, but whatever it was, they certainly weren't giving up easily. If the Black pirate was anything to go by, the Bandi were even more bloodthirsty and ruthless than Captain Red. I just hoped and prayed we could outrun them.

Chapter 22

Takootu's Trick

The cannons continued to roar and deafen us, as we raced across the water aboard the *Captain Cook*. The sea exploded around us as the cannon balls showered down from the clear blue sky. Some of the smaller boats capsised as large waves reared up and unbalanced them. A number of the crew were thrown into the choppy waters, but were swiftly rescued by the brave Radi battle canoes.

Miraculously, none of the Radi boats had been directly hit. Not yet at any rate …

The Radi villagers looked out nervously from their small fishing boats. They were no match for the power and might of the Bandi fighting ships and Takootu knew it.

Suddenly he gave another signal to the Radi fleet. Almost instantaneously, the Radi craft started to spread out in all directions, making it much more difficult for the Bandi to target them with their cannons. It was a masterstroke by Takootu. The Bandi didn't know which vessel to follow or fire on, but they still kept on chasing.

The Radi warriors kept paddling as fast as they could and the villagers in their fishing boats used all their sailing skills and knowledge of the local winds, as they tried to distance themselves from the Bandi guns.

"They're still close to us!" cried Tametoa, anxiously. "Keep going, everyone!"

Takootu looked concerned and fired out more instructions to us all in an attempt to win us a bit more speed. Thankfully it seemed to work. We started to pull away slowly. But he wasn't just concerned about the *Captain Cook*. He was constantly looking nervously around - port and starboard - to check how the rest of his fleet was fairing.

After a long, tense and nervous chase, we were astonished to find ourselves out in open water - the sounds of the cannons were a distant rumble...

We had ESCAPED!

We just hoped that the whole of the Radi fleet had managed to escape unharmed as well.

As we drew closer to Radimatu, we started to see more and more fishing boats and battle canoes emerge from all directions. We waved to each other excitedly. It looked like Takootu's 'trick' had WORKED - we had managed to outrun the Bandi!

Takootu looked tired, but his smile was full of joy and relief. He raised his Rodu again towards the fleet to acknowledge their great bravery and courage. His smile shone out like a beacon - full of gratitude and warmth to his wonderful Radi people.

All of a sudden we noticed a large shoal of dolphins approaching in the water...

"Poe!" screamed Rai, excitedly, as her loyal friendly

dolphin soared out of the water in front of us, squeaking noisily.

"Puati!" cried Mareva, eagerly, as she spotted her favourite friend spinning acrobatically through the air.

Soon they were both alongside the *Captain Cook* escorting us back to Radimatu – in fact the whole shoal of ten or more was with us.

"They saved my life," said Tametoa earnestly, waving to them both affectionately, and throwing up some fish for them into the sky. "They kept me going, when I got tired. I'm not sure I would have made it without them…"

Tametoa suddenly looked very emotional. It must have been a huge physical and mental test for him swimming that long distance home to Radimatu, but thankfully for us all he had managed it. He had saved all our lives.

We all gave Tametoa a massive hug and thanked him again for being so brave.

"What's the BIG deal everybody?" joked Nino, giving

Tametoa a warm brotherly embrace. "I could have swum it with my eyes closed!"

"Yeah, yeah!" smiled Rai, rolling her eyes. "Of course you could have, Nino. And with your hands tied behind your back too, right?"

"Exactly," replied Nino, with a smirk.

We all laughed. It was comforting to see Nino back making silly jokes. After the horror and heartache of the past few days, life suddenly felt more normal once again.

Poe and Puati continued to entertain us with a multitude of tricks, as we were escorted back into the harbour. Minoo looked most impressed. He was chattering away excitedly and then started to do somersaults and back flips of his own.

"I think he wants to be a dolphin too!" laughed Jana, affectionately. "Great spin, Minoo!"

As we drew closer to shore we could see a large crowd of villagers gathered around the harbour wall cheering and waving excitedly. I peered through my telescope eagerly and there was Grandma, Grandad, Mum and Dad, right at the front , waiting to greet us! Soon we would be having one of our biggest family hugs EVER...

I could still hardly believe that we had escaped. We were almost home now - soon we would be back at Radimatu and safe once more.

Chapter 23

Home-Coming

That evening we had a huge Tahitian feast to celebrate our safe return. None of us had eaten for the last few days so we were all starving. It was so good to be back with everyone again, and the fresh fruit salad and vanilla coconut milk shakes were extremely YUMMY! Mum and Dad looked very relieved to have us back safe and sound, but we knew we were in for a bit of a ticking off.

"We were all so worried about you," said Mum, getting tearful again. "Anything could have happened to you…"

 "Yes … ANYTHING and all of it BAD," added Dad, still sounding very upset. "Please don't just go off like that again."

"No Jay and Jana!" added Grandma, her voice quivering with emotion. "Don't ever dream of it! Please, we were so…"

Grandma suddenly stopped speaking, tears started streaming down her rosy red cheeks and she hugged us both close to her.

"I'm not letting you go 'til you promise…" she whispered softly.

We promised we wouldn't and she eventually let us go, but only after hugging us for at least another minute or two. Grandad went on to say how brave we both had been to go and help try and win back the treasure.

"Not brave," added Grandma curtly. "FOOLISH more like! You could have been lost out at sea for years or even worse…"

Grandma was right, we had been a bit crazy. We just didn't think it was going to be THAT dangerous. We had been lucky to get through it in one piece.

We were all feeling exhausted now, but Grandma and

Grandad weren't looking tired at all.

"Tell us more about your adventure," asked Grandad excitedly. I want to hear all about the volcano blowing again and your battles with Captain Red..."

"And I want another spin with my wonderful dance partner!" smiled Grandma, warmly. "Come on Minoo..."

Chapter 24

Takootu's Treasure

The next day it was the opening of the Museum and we were the special guests. It was the day after Zeo's day, but all the villagers had been given an extra day's special holiday and had come out in their hundreds to celebrate.

We were all still feeling very disappointed about losing Zeo's Treasure, especially as it was supposed to be the main attraction of the Museum opening. But thankfully, the islanders were in a jubilant mood after the remarkable rescue. Takootu, their extraordinary and much-adored chief, and his entire family were now all back safe in Radimatu - when they could have been lost forever.

After we had officially opened the Museum, Takootu started to address the huge crowd. He spoke to his people in his native language, adding bits in English, so we could understand what he was saying too. Mareva translated the rest for us.

He thanked the entire Radi fleet for coming out in their boats to help make our incredible rescue possible. He thanked all the Radi warriors for fighting so valiantly to help recapture the treasure, despite them not succeeding.

After each 'thank you' that Takootu made, the crowd cheered loudly and threw colourful flowers into the warm summer air. Last of all he thanked his four amazing children, and Jana, me and Minoo for everything we had done.

"You is all very special to me," he continued, sounding quite emotional. "Thank you. I is so proud of you and I is sure that Zeo is proud of you too."

The crowd cheered loudly again and threw more brightly-coloured flowers into the air. We felt very honoured to receive such praise and waved back at the huge crowd shyly, with a warm feeling welling up inside us.

We thought that was the end of his speech, but Takootu wasn't finished. There was more...

The island Elders had decided to reward Tametoa with a special award for showing incredible bravery as he swam the long distance back to Radimatu.

Takootu watched on proudly, with a tear in his eye, as the Elders presented him with a *Pukui*. Mareva explained that the *Pukui* was an exceptional type of Rodu, made from ancient wood of incredible quality and only given to warriors who showed extraordinary courage.

Heartfelt cheers of appreciation rang out from the Radi villagers. Tametoa's courage had saved us all. Takootu wiped the tears from his eyes as the two warriors who had saved his life stepped up next to receive the same distinguished award.

After the crowd's cheers had subsided once more, Takootu continued with his speech. He started to talk about Zeo's Treasure and what he said was quite a surprise to us all...

"The treasure is almost costing lives of my family and your families too. I is thinking maybe it is being more trouble than it is worth...? There is crazy peoples out there who is stopping at nothing... "

Some of the villagers murmured softly in agreement, but others were sounding disappointed, including Tametoa who started to look clearly angry and upset.

"I'm never giving up on Zeo's Treasure," he hissed, "Whatever Papa say's – it's part of our history!"

"Me neither," agreed Nino, enthusiastically. "We can't

give it up now…!"

"Quiet, you two!" ordered Mareva, sternly. "Trust Papa to do the right thing for our island and people…"

Nino and Tametoa fell silent as Takootu continued to address the huge crowd.

"Tomorrow, Radi Elders is meeting. We discuss treasure. Where is it? We not knowing for sure. Maybe on ocean floor in wreck of *Golden Age*? If so, maybe we is deciding to try to recover it. We have best pearl divers in Polynesia here in Radimatu – so maybe it is being possible. Yes?"

Takootu turned towards Mareva and Rai and winked cheerfully.

The crowd murmured expectantly.

"But maybe Captain Red not drowning…" continued Takootu, in a serious tone. "Maybe he is alive and he takes treasure to Bandi hideout far far away from here…"

The crowd gasped disappointedly. They hadn't been prepared for this possible outcome.

"Yes it is bad news my friends… maybe very bad news… and I is sorry to bring it to you," continued Takootu, sensing his people's mood. "But I is now bringing you little bit of good news too…"

A buzz went around the villagers.

"If treasure still with Captain Red and Bandi – we know where they is taking it!"

Takootu held up a scrap of paper triumphantly to show the crowd. The scrap of paper which Minoo had rescued from Captain Red's top jacket pocket – the

CHART!

"We is having the MAP to lead us there!" declared Takootu, beaming from ear to ear. "Thanks to brave, clever monkey and all of these young heroes!"

The crowd gasped again, but this time in hope and anticipation. Takootu pushed us all forward to receive the cheers and adulation of the islanders once more. Then the Elders presented us all with our own special awards.

Minoo received a huge basket of grapes which he tucked into immediately. The rest of us all received beautifully designed pendants, handmade by craftspeople from the island. Mine was shaped like a spiral, and Jana's was fashioned like an exotic flower.

Mareva explained that the pendants were not only stunning, but were known to bring good luck and bestow special powers to the wearer.

If we were ever to run into Captain Red again on a future adventure, some good luck and extra special powers could certainly come in VERY handy. The crowd eventually stopped applauding and cheering for us, and we all thought that was the end of the presentation, but Takootu STILL hadn't finished...

"I is having one more thing to say... it is last thing and I am thinking it is being most important for us all..."

There was an instant hush. The Radi had a tremendous respect and admiration for their Chief, and they could tell that he had something very important to say.

"We may never be seeing treasure again. It is possible and I know you is all being sad about it like me – it is part of our heritage – but please do not be TOO sad. Look around you. We is all being blessed by Zeo's love. We is living on beautiful island – with family and friends who is caring for us and loving us. Is this not 'treasure' enough for any peoples?"

The crowd was silent for a few seconds, as though what Takootu had said was just sinking in...

Then suddenly the villagers started to cheer even louder than they had cheered before and threw even more colourful flowers into the air. Then everyone started to hug each other, as though they had just been given a very special gift and wanted to share it with the person next to them.

It was a wonderful ending to a very special day.

We joined in the hugging too - BIG time! Grandma started by giving us all one of her legendary HUMONGOUS hugs – including Takootu!

Everyone seemed so HAPPY...!!

I threw Minoo up in the air and caught him like I always did. That set Nino off. He started pretending to be Minoo – standing on his head, squeaking and pulling silly faces...

Then Minoo joined in too, and suddenly there was a

competition for who could pull the funniest face and make the silliest noise. We all started to laugh and giggle and that made Nino and Minoo do it even MORE!

Takootu was right. We were all very lucky to be surrounded by people we loved and to be living on a beautiful island. And we were determined to make the most of the rest of our holiday.

We still had six more weeks living as Takootu's special guests on his wonderful Polynesian Island. Six more weeks to explore every inch of Radimatu, with Takootu, Nino, Rai, Tametoa and Mareva as our very own tour guides.

Six more weeks FREE of maths and spellings tests...

Six more weeks of fun and games with all the family, but especially with MINOO! Climbing palm trees just like last year and maybe even climbing up the volcano – as long as it wasn't LIVE...!

Takootu would be meeting with the Radi Elders tomorrow to decide what to do next about the treasure.

But somehow I already felt certain that this was not the end of Zeo's Treasure, or our astonishing adventures in the South Pacific…

Dear Reader

I hope you enjoyed this book? If you did, please write me a book review at www.amazon.co.uk. I would love to hear what you think about the story and the characters. Thanks you.

Also, look out for the next adventure in the series – it's coming soon!

Best wishes
Chris Davies

Books by Christopher Davies

If you would like to find out about the author, please check out the Author's Page for Christopher Davies on amazon.co.uk

(Chris on a family walking holiday in Canada.)

Books by Christopher Davies

If you would like to find out about or purchase other books written by the author, please check out the Author's Page for Christopher Davies on amazon.co.uk

Books available include:

'Prickly-Pong Island & the Emerald Treasure'

A swashbuckling, green-themed adventure set in the islands of the South Pacific! Monkeys, pirates and Prickly-Pong! Age 7+

'In a Spin'   An exciting school based dance adventure - full of twists and turns! 8+

'Times Table Time & Rhyme' Catchy amusing rhymes to help make learning your times tables easy and enjoyable! Themes include: Sweets, football, snow, baking a cake, & trips to the zoo, the seaside and the school disco. Age 5+

Prickly-Pong Island & the Emerald Treasure

TREASURE is a wonderful thing... but is it more important than anything?

Jay finds school difficult but his twin sister Sanjana loves it - so when Dad wins a holiday to a desert island, Jay thinks all his dreams have come true! Maths and spellings tests are happily replaced with climbing palm trees and making friends with the mischievous monkeys.

But living in an island paradise doesn't turn out to be all fun & games and before long, Jay and Sanjana become entangled in a daring real-life escapade they would never have believed possible! Pirates and 'Prickly-Pong' - lost treasure and tattooed tribes. Life soon becomes VERY different from school! Danger is lurking everywhere - something far more terrifying than the most menacing pirate...

A thrilling 'green-themed' adventure set in the islands of the South-Pacific. Full of humour & happiness; sadness & regret; bravery & friendship. 7+

"My 7 year old son absolutely loved this story... A perfect mix of adventure and suspense. He didn't want it to end and can't wait for the next one in the series." Lucy

In a Spin

It's almost time! The annual St. George's Dance Competition is only days away. Maddy is favourite to win but something serious is bothering her...

Close friend, Jack is a daring Break-Dancer who is going all out to beat his arch rival Justin, but will Jack's fiery temper get the better of him?

All the twists and turns you could wish for in this lively, action-packed, School Dance drama. Age 8+

"This book is amazing. After reading the first couple of chapters I wanted to read all of it straight away! The character of Maddy is my favourite as she loves dancing like me and I like the end of term dance competition... I loved the ending because it was surprising. I would give it loads more than 5 stars if I could!"
Lottie (Age 9)

The Revenge of Captain Red

The Revenge of Captain Red

The Revenge of Captain Red

The Revenge of Captain Red

The Revenge of Captain Red

Printed in Great Britain
by Amazon